Vanishing
Act

Books by
Dorothy Nafus Morrison

Whisper Goodbye
Somebody's Horse
Whisper Again
Vanishing Act

VANISHING

*ACT

Dorothy Nafus Morrison

Atheneum   *1989*   *New York*

For John and Lynne
and Steven
D. N. M.

Atheneum
Macmillan Publishing Company
866 Third Avenue, New York, NY 10022
Collier Macmillan Canada, Inc.
Designed by Kimberly M. Hauck
First Edition
Printed in the United States of America
10   9   8   7   6   5   4   3   2   1

Library of Congress Cataloging-in-Publication Data
Morrison, Dorothy Nafus.
Vanishing act/Dorothy Nafus Morrison.
—1st ed.   p.   cm.
Summary: While researching tricks for the magic act she is
planning for her junior high school talent show, Jo finds a
strange device that can make objects vanish, but she does not
realize how dangerous it can be until she accidentally
turns herself invisible.
ISBN 0–689–31513–9
[1. Magic—Fiction.   2. Magic tricks—Fiction.]   I. Title.
PZ7. M8293Van   1989   [Fic]—dc19
88–36026   CIP   AC

Contents

The Way
It Started

IF JOANNA RODGERS HAD KNOWN HOW POW-
erful magic could be—that she might totally, ut-
terly, absolutely disappear—she wouldn't have
begged Mr. Paisley to let her into the back room
of his shop. She wouldn't have taken a single step
through the dark little door that was generally kept
locked, or poked around in the rolltop desk, or
found what was hidden in its bottom drawer. But
until the day she discovered the desk, Jo had
caught only an occasional glimpse of the vast, high-
ceilinged storage area, extending out and out
over the cold water of Madrona Bay. She had no
idea what was there.

All her thoughts were about the weekend, on that

Friday afternoon in March when she sat in her classroom in Madrona Junior High with her books stacked, ready to leave. Just before the final bell, the door opened and the drama coach, Miss Hall, breezed in.

"Hi, folks! I have an announcement!" she exclaimed, high heels tapping across the floor. Miss Hall was lively and slender, with bright brown eyes and wavy hair tied back with a scarf. The kids liked her.

"A tryout for an all-school talent show, a week from today," she continued in her ringing, cheerleader voice. "Any of you can enter, and offer any act you want—within the bounds of decency, of course." She rolled her eyes toward the right, toward the left, as if letting the students in on a private joke.

Somebody in the back corner snickered, and then others did, too, while Jo slid farther forward in her seat. Talent show! All-school! She glanced across the aisle to her best friend, Kim Eberly, but Kim was looking straight ahead.

Miss Hall held up her hand for silence. "Music will be fine. A skit ... dance ... whatever ... and the three best will be in the main performance at the high school, on the following Friday evening." She folded her arms. "I'm counting on you to represent us well."

Jo had been fascinated with magic ever since she

first learned it in Mr. Paisley's summer class in the park. Right from the start she had taken to it—silks to flourish, crisp cards slipping through her fingers, a coin hidden behind her thumb. Besides having strong, limber hands that easily mastered the props, she practiced every day, and soon became Mr. Paisley's star pupil. Before long she was asked to put on magic shows for children's birthday parties, and that was fun—standing in front of an audience, surprising them, making them laugh. Her brother, Woody, was a computer shark, but now she had a special thing, too, one that she loved and was extra good at.

"Kim! Let's enter!" she whispered, leaning into the aisle, for she and Kim had begun to work as a team.

"On the *stage*? In front of the *whole school*?" Kim whispered back, with a glance of alarm.

"Sure. We can do it," Jo insisted.

Kim twisted a lock of her curly red hair, and drew down the corners of her mouth. "Yuk-k-k!"

"It's our first chance at a really big show! It'll be fun!" Miss Hall was looking at them, so Jo sat up straight, but her mind was far off, scrabbling around possible tricks for the tryout. Unbeatable Drum ... Dragon Puppet ... Dancing Handkerchiefs. Although she had often been embarrassed because she was so long-legged and bony, all knees and elbows, she now imagined herself crisp and professional on the high-school stage. The audience would cheer. The Madrona Merlins—the magic club of which she was president—would be proud of her. Mr. Paisley had already hinted that she might be his summer assistant, and when he saw her big act, he'd be sure to give her the job. She might—Jo caught her breath—she might even become famous.

Later, while they were waiting for the school bus, Jo brought up the tryout again. "We can do it!" she insisted.

"You think so?" Kim drew her lips down in a grimace of disgust. "Who needs it?"

"I do!"

"Uh-uh!"

But Jo persisted, and just as the school bus lumbered around the corner, Kim gave a grudging consent.

As soon as Jo got home, she ran up to her own room, which she had done in silver and deep blue, the colors of magic. She laid all her equipment on the bed to help in planning the act, and when her parents came home, she met them with a flood of talk about Miss Hall's announcement.

"Can you put off your trip?" she asked when she had finished, for they owned a gift shop and were about to leave for Europe on their annual buying expedition.

"Not a chance," her father replied, his dark eyes

sober. Tall and lanky like Jo, he almost always found time to watch her new tricks and tell her which ones worked. "If we'd known about it a month ago . . ."

"We'd like to," added her mother, who had made her a magician's cloak. "But we can't possibly change our reservations—flights, hotels, some special showings. And Mrs. Forbes is all ready to move in."

"Cookbooks, TV guides and all!" Jo replied, giving them a grin. Mrs. Forbes, who was the assistant at their gift shop, had stayed with Jo and her brother, Woody, so many times that she seemed almost like one of the family.

Her mother was still troubled. "Jo . . . we'd love to watch you try out. If if weren't for this trip . . ."

"It's all right—honest," Jo replied. Nothing could bother her right then. Long after she went to bed, she imagined herself onstage while the kids, Woody, the teachers sat on the edges of their seats and wondered how she could work such astonishing tricks. First thing in the morning, she'd go to Mr. Paisley's shop, the Druid's Cave, and ask him to help her figure out the best routine ever.

The next day she hurried through breakfast, and when her parents left for their shop, she rode with them, down the long hill to Old Main Street.

Madrona was a former fishing village on the Oregon coast. Forested mountains loomed above the roofs on one side of the street, while on the other side, toward Madrona Bay, the black spars of fishing boats swayed against the brilliant blue sky. Here, in this old section, many of the shops had old-fashioned wide porches, or rear decks which rested on massive wooden pilings and extended over the water. They had been repaired and painted for the tourist trade, white or blue or yellow, with pointed gables and bay windows—like a village in a fairy tale, Jo often thought.

She loved Old Town, but today she merely hopped out of the station wagon and hurried along the street until she came to a dark gray building with a swinging wooden sign that said DRUID'S CAVE: SKY HIGH. Here she bounded onto the porch, lifted the black iron latch, and walked in.

It was a double store with the Druid's Cave on one side and a kite shop called Sky High on the other. They were connected by a short hallway, and Jo turned toward the left, passing a row of magicians' birdcages on pedestals and a table of small tricks.

"Mr. Paisley?" The quiet of the Cave, its dark walls, the heaviness of its low ceiling seemed to fold over her, and she blinked in the gloom. It was small and crowded, lighted by three bare bulbs close to the ceiling, and its air was dry, with a faint, dusty smell, like attics or old trunks. Nothing moved. There was no sound. "Mr. Paisley?"

she asked again, almost in a whisper. Could he be in the back room? "Hello!"

A fishing boat sounded its hoarse whistle, after which the Cave was still again.

"Mr. Paisley?" she repeated, a little louder. "Is anybody here?"

"Ah! Our young friend!" a voice rasped, as a wiry young man ambled down the hallway between shops. He was Sidney Larrance, owner of Sky High, and he and Mr. Paisley sometimes helped one another. "My humble services are yours to command." He made a deep bow, sweeping one hand in a wide arc and raising his eyebrows into arches, pointed like tents.

"I'm looking for Mr. Paisley. I want to ask him something," Jo replied, disappointed. Sidney was fun—a tease, lively, full of wry jokes—and all the kids liked him, but she didn't want to spend her precious time with him now.

"No problem! Your mentor is out back, assaying his treasures. He'll be with you directly." Sidney rumpled his hair, which was thick and ragged, danging over his collar. "But you're agitated. Out of breath. Need any help from faithful Sid?"

Jo tried to sound casual. "Not really. I just want to tell him that I'm going to be in a really big show."

"Ah! That's enough to give anyone's eyes a glitter." Sidney grinned, which parted his straggly mustache. "But I hear our host, so my services won't be needed after all." With a quick wave, he strode back down the hall, footsteps slapping on the wooden floor.

Just as he left, a narrow, dark door in the rear wall opened, and Mr. Paisley shuffled through, carrying a large box. Small, gray-haired and bent, he lurked like a spider in his dark little shop; and as he walked, he turned his head from side to side, gazing over the tops of his half-moon glasses.

"There you are!" Jo exclaimed, hurrying across the floor to meet him. "Something really great has happened!"

"Why—Joanna," he replied in a voice that was soft and deep, with a buzz like a distant bee. Balancing the box on one hand, he fumbled in his pocket for a set of keys and locked the narrow door; but before it closed, Jo caught a glimpse of the other room, dark and high, stretching far back toward the harbor.

"Let me get rid of this," he continued, "and then I want to hear all about it." Humming his buzzy hum, he took the box to the counter where he kept materials for packaging. Jo followed along, and as he pulled out a ledger and made an entry, she heard him murmur, "Alexis De Jong, Las Vegas." He closed the ledger and looked up at Jo. "It has to make the mail this afternoon."

Las Vegas! With its super shows! Jo thought. Siegfried and Roy were there, and other famous magicians, too. The Druid's Cave was said to be the finest magic shop on the entire coast, and now Mr. Paisley was sending a trick to somebody in Las Vegas!

After replacing the ledger, he shuffled toward Jo. "I made you wait, and that was too bad. But now we have time. So—something has happened?" he asked.

"Oh! You'll never guess! I'm going to be in a really big show. That is, in a tryout." Her words were tumbling over one another. "They're going to have three winners. And I want ..."

"Slowly, slowly. But first, let's make ourselves comfortable." With small, quick steps, he led her to the rear corner, which held a round, potbellied stove, its fire bright behind four squares of glass. Several wooden chairs with arms were clustered around it, and Mr. Paisley motioned her to one, dropped into another, then leaned forward and spread out his wrinkled hands to the heat. "Now— what has happened to give you such shining eyes?"

As clearly as she could, trying not to talk in exclamation points, Jo told him what Miss Hall had said. "And *please* help me figure out what to do," she finished.

"You want to test your mettle. Of course. Perhaps ... a friend?" His faded blue eyes twinkled as he touched Jo's sleeve—and his hand held a stuffed mouse made of white velvet, with pink eyes and tail. "Have you something for Anthony? A bit of cheese? He's waiting!"

Jo rubbed the little creature's stomach and giggled as its mechanical whiskers began to quiver. She had seen it often, because Mr. Paisely almost always carried it with him, to entertain children. "He's cute. But our talent show will be for adults," she said.

"Of course. We can do better than Anthony." Mr. Paisley tucked the mouse into his pocket, took out a deck of cards, and handed them to her. "So, have you been practicing the Double Fan? It was going well, last week."

Jo ran the deck through a rapid shuffle. "Yes, and I've almost got it, I think." Biting her lip in concentration, she pulled off some cards, gave them two flips, and held them up in a rough but fanlike formation. "It's a little better, anyway," she said. "I've been working on it a lot."

"That I can see," he told her with a smile, taking back the cards. "Unfortunately they won't show up onstage. But perhaps some Dancing Silks?" He waved his arm and a shiny green square was billowing up and down at his fingertips, sweeping to one side, to the other, higher, lower. Everything was still, except the blast of a whistle as another fishing boat passed.

"Mr. Paisley," Jo said in a few minutes, "that looks just wonderful, and I think I'll try some silk tricks.

Some easy ones. But I want something that's really superspecial. I've checked what you have out here, lots of times, and now I wish—can I look back there? Please?" She bobbed her head toward the narrow door in the rear wall.

"What, pray, do you find so intriguing about my storage room?" he asked, his smile fading.

"You told me once that you keep your most advanced tricks there; and that box, the one for somebody in Las Vegas, must be extra special. So ..."

Serious now, his twinkle gone, Mr. Paisley crumpled the green silk and stuffed it into his pocket. "There's nothing for you back there, Joanna. Only the devices I keep on hand for professionals, plus kiddie tricks for my beginners' table. The one you saw, for De Jong, is high-quality Billiard Balls, and your hands aren't big enough to manipulate them, even if you had the skill."

"But ... please?"

Mr. Paisley lifted his shoulders in a heavy sigh. "You won't find anything helpful in the storeroom, and you're hoodwinking yourself if you depend on mechanical tricks. How you present them—that's what matters." He sat back and made a tent of his fingers, looking thoughtfully at her. "I want you to do well, Joanna. And ..." He gave her the enigmatic smile again. "I'm counting on you, perhaps this summer...."

Counting on her! "I'll try. I'll do my very best,"

Jo promised, not daring to ask what he meant. If he chose her to be his student assistant, she could work with magic all summer, and go to the Magicians' Fair in the fall!

"Splendid. You must choose a suitable character for this tryout, and develop your act around that. Such as—let's see—Merlin? You had a Merlin costume once, as I remember."

"I still do. But Merlin is so *common*!"

"A visiting lecturer? Mad scientist? Clown?"

"Not those. But . . ." Jo thought of the equipment she had laid out on her bed. "Maybe my magician's cloak? The one Mom made me?"

"Of course!" Mr. Paisley beamed. "A traditional magician, doing a classic routine. It suits you well."

"What tricks . . ."

He held up his hand. "If I tell you that, it will be my act, not yours, so you must think your hardest, and decide what you do best. Except . . ." Grasping the arms of his chair, he shoved himself to his feet. "I'll give you one new thing, Joanna. If it works, fine. If not, we'll find another."

Slippers scraping on the floor, he went to a corner shelf and brought back a box labeled "Growth Accelerator." "No—no charge," he insisted when she took out her wallet. "It's a gift, for luck."

"Mr. Paisley! A brand-new trick! I'm sure it will be just right! I'll practice with it a lot!"

"Good. Come again in a few days, and see if you

can fool me." He waved from the door as she left.

For all the rest of the week, Jo spent every possible moment developing her act. She experimented with the Growth Accelerator and found that she could make a stuffed baby rabbit seem to grow instantly into an adult. She wrote out patter and went over it until she could almost say it in her sleep. She practiced in front of her mirror, and her brother, Woody—a year older and in the ninth grade—listened patiently and told her what worked best. She rehearsed with Kim, who giggled and pretended to be dumb—a perfect assistant.

On Tuesday Jo washed her white shirt, pressed her black pants and magician's cloak, tried them on and looked into the long mirror. Had she really wished to be little and curvy like Kim? Surely not, for this was much better—tall, perhaps a bit knobby, but just right for her act. Mysterious. Intense.

On Wednesday after school she went to the Cave, to show Mr. Paisley the entire routine, and in the evening she did it for her parents.

"It's really very good, Jo," said her mother, who had taken time out from packing for their trip.

"Class act," her father agreed.

On Thursday Jo's parents left, and when she returned from school that afternoon she found that Mrs. Forbes had already moved in, bringing three large suitcases, a tote bag full of knitting needles and yarn, a stack of cookbooks, and a television set on a stand that she could roll from room to room.

Before Jo went to bed that night, she packed her equipment into a suitcase and a large corrugated box, ready to take to school.

And then it was Friday, April 4. The day of the tryout had come.

Joanna
of the
Black Cloak

THE DAY AT SCHOOL ALTERNATELY RACED AND dragged. Sometimes when Jo looked at the clock, then looked again, the hands had scarcely moved. At other times they seemd to spin—five after—ten—twenty—while her stomach turned somersaults and her heart thumped. "Hello, everybody, I've brought you some mysterious rings," she silently recited. In a little while she'd be onstage, doing the act she'd been dreaming about all week. Then why was she so shaky? Once she got started, it would be fun as magic always was, like riding a wave, or floating on the wind. It was only the waiting that was so hard.

Would two o'clock ever come?

But somehow, after an eternity, the hours had passed, school had been dismissed early, and Jo was standing in the wings of the auditorium, wrinkling her nose against the dust. She glanced down at her magician's cloak, touched her high, white collar and black bow tie, and patted her coattails to feel the colored silks that were hidden in the secret pockets.

"Is my makeup on straight?" she whispered to Kim, who was standing at her elbow.

"Perfect," Kim whispered back, smoothing her bright pink miniskirt and jacket. The freckles stood out on her pale cheeks, and she was trembling. "Jo—my knees have positively turned to Jell-O."

Jo took hold of her hand. "We'll be all right; just hang on." It was starting—it was here. In a few minutes she'd walk into the lights, and she wouldn't be Jo Rodgers, student, but Joanna of the Black Cloak, Magician.

Staring at the polished wooden floor, she silently repeated the advice her teachers had been pouring out to her. *Stand tall. Look at what you want your audiences to see, not at what you're doing. Smile, no matter what!*

She whispered her diction exercises. "P-p-p-p-p-p. Peter piper picked a peck of ... T-t-t-t. K-k-k-k."

While the boy at the piano played a rippling run

followed by some heavy chords, Jo peeked around the edge of the curtain, and her stomach plunged. The auditorium was full! Besides the students, lots of adults had come, too, and were sitting at the back. She closed her eyes. *Stand tall! Look at what you . . .*

And then, all in a rush, the boy at the piano was bowing, people were clapping, and Miss Hall slipped an arm around Jo's waist. "Time to begin," she said, in her heartiest voice. "Good luck." She gave Jo and Kim each a pat on the shoulder.

"Thanks!" Jo managed a smile, while the student stagehands carried her magician's stand and Kim's table into place. "Ready?" she whispered to Kim, as she heard a booming voice on the loudspeaker.

"Our next contestant—Joanna Rodgers, Magician. Assisted by Kim Eberly."

They walked onto the stage.

The lights were ten times, a hundred times as bright as Jo expected, making her squint. In the glare she could barely see the audience, just the first few rows of faces staring up at her, all eyes and toothy grins. She caught a glimpse of her magic club, the Madrona Merlins, sitting together at one side, and Woody, in the front row, slumped as usual onto the end of his backbone. But she hadn't long to look, for the house grew quiet and it was time to start.

"Okay!" She nodded to Kim, who fluffed out her skirt, and handed over the Linking Rings.

Jo had decided to open with this trick because she had done it for so many birthday parties, and audiences liked it. "Hello, everybody! I've something special here," she began.

Speak out! she reminded herself. *The ones in back want to hear, too.* She glanced at Woody, but he was looking away and twisting his knuckles. Was he ashamed? He'd told her a thousand times that she twittered like a chicken, and maybe she was doing that now. Jo cleared her throat and tried again, as loudly as she could. "*As you can see, each Ring is separate from all the rest.*" She showed the Rings, put them behind her back, brought them out as a chain—and the students clapped. She'd made good start, and suddenly the show was fun again.

She bobbed her head toward Kim, who trotted across the stage with the colored silks. They danced up and down, smooth and swishing as they should, and Jo's hands stopped trembling. When she rolled her eyes and gave her shoulders an exaggerated shrug, she heard a ripple of laughter, so she twitched her shoulders again, feeling like a seasoned performer.

"And now I have a brand-new invention! A Growth Accelerator!" she exclaimed, picking up the trick Mr. Paisley had given her. "Empty." She turned it so everyone could see. "But if I put in a baby rabbit, he will grow up at once." She turned toward Kim. "Have we a baby rabbit?"

"Oh, yes! Right here!" Kim quavered, as she

brought over the small stuffed animal.

"*Thank* you!" Jo put the little rabbit into the box, turned on the motor sound, and a moment later reached in confidently for a large, brown rabbit, the kind called a "kicker" because it could move as if it were alive. However, she somehow didn't press the inflation button firmly enough, and instead of popping out plump and wiggly with its ears pricked, the rabbit hung from her hand, as limp as an old sock.

"It's . . . it's . . ." She'd bobbled it! Should she press the button now? No, the kids would notice. Start over? Surely not! Everybody had seen the big rabbit and would know it was a fake. Mr. Paisley had often told her that if a trick went wrong, she should either repeat it or begin another at once, so she stuffed the rabbit back into the accelerator. "Let's see the . . ." She bent over to read her list, which was pasted to the edge of her stand, and somebody at the back of the hall snickered.

They were laughing at her! Jo stood up again. "It didn't . . . didn't!" *What was next?* She heard another giggle. Looking frantically toward Kim, and seeing the Unbeatable Drum on the side table, she blurted out, "How about a drum solo?"

"Oh—sure!" Kim's feet clattered on the bare floor as she carried over the drum and drumstick, and Jo took them with shaking hands. *Lighten up!* she told herself as she gave the drum a thump and broke its paper head, as she intended. But somehow, when she turned it over to beat the other side, she dropped it, and the stack of flattened dolls, which were supposed to be a surprise later on, came sliding out.

As Jo looked at the drum on the floor, surrounded by the tangle of dolls, an echoing, cold, black tunnel seemed to open up in front of her, and all of a sudden her mind went blank. For the first time in any show, she couldn't remember a single trick or a word of patter. All those people were waiting and laughing, and she couldn't think of anything except a wish to run off the stage into a closet where she could hide and never show her face again.

Wiping her sweaty hands on her coattails, she glanced toward Miss Hall, who was standing in the wings with a determined smile on her face. "It's okay, Jo. Super. Just settle down!" she hissed.

"I'll try," Jo whispered back, so loudly that somebody laughed again.

Jo doubled her fists. She wasn't going to stop, not now! Sometimes the plans of real magicians didn't work out quite right, but they kept going. So she'd do the ... the ... She gave Kim a frantic glance, and there, on the assistant's table, was another silk, a large blue one. Of course! Her old standby, Handkerchief Tinder, which she had done a dozen—twenty—a hundred times. That couldn't possibly go wrong. "Kim! The Tinder!" she said.

"Right!" After rummaging in the supply box,

Kim scuttled toward Jo's table with the Tinder equipment.

Now keep cool! Jo told herself. This is easy. Forcing herself to take a deep, calm breath, she shook out the handkerchief and folded it around the hidden thumb tip, which was made of metal and shaped like a thimble.

"Fire, fire, bright and hot; flicker, flicker, burn it not!" she chanted as she lighted a match and plunged it into the fold, where the thumb tip would shield it. "Look closely, everybody, at the magic square, still as good as new. See how it has been guarded by its Good Genie. See how ..." With her best flourish she pulled the handkerchief free—and its center had developed a charred, brown hole.

Jo felt like a jellyfish that had been washed up on the beach and stepped on. She'd been lying awake nights, imagining herself famous, imagining the kids perched on the edges of their seats, mouths open with astonishment. Well, they were open-mouthed, all right, giggling, smirking—all those she could see. Miss Hall walked out in front, flapped her hands above her head and shouted, "That's enough—*enough*! Quiet, everybody!" But the kids continued to titter, while Kim burst into sobs and ran offstage.

Jo was left alone in the glare of the light. Forcing her lips into a smile as stiff as plywood, she hugged her arms across her stomach and blinked against the tears that were making everything a blur. But *that* won't help, she stormed to herself. Kim might be scared off, but for her part, she wouldn't. She positively *wouldn't quit*! She'd do something! Anything would be better than standing there as silent as a clam!

"So you think it's funny!" she quavered. "Okay! Laugh!" Her voice was growing louder. *"Maybe it is!"*

She didn't know quite how it happened, but at that second, as she put on another plywood smile, her voice became strong and clear. "Well! Trouble again! Something seems to have gone wrong!" she called out. "Let's see if . . . if we can . . ." Her voice was still louder. *"If we can figure it out!"* She turned the handkerchief around and around, looking behind it and in front of it, pretending she'd lost something.

The snickers quieted down.

Instead of fighting tears, Jo was suddenly burning with anger, as if her insides had all caught fire. Savagely she thrust a finger through the charred hole and wiggled it back and forth, pursing her lips into a round O of astonishment. *They weren't going to drive her away.* Making believe the handkerchief was hot, she groaned, jerked her finger free and put it into her mouth. "I'm blistered!" she exclaimed in a voice that cracked like that of a Halloween witch. "Woe! Woe is me!"

Although someone giggled again, it was a different, friendly sound. *That's right! Let them laugh!* Jo thought. And if they liked this disgusting funny business, she'd keep on acting like a fool!

She sniffed at the hole, poked her nose through, curled her lips into mock dismay. She picked up the rabbit, pretended to weep, wiped her eyes with the rabbit's ears and put on a show of wringing them out. *"This* is *awful,"* she chanted in the deepest singsong she could; and she heard a spatter of applause while Kim, ashen-pale, tiptoed back to the table.

"Bravo!" "Atta girl!" voices shouted.

Calm and cold, Jo worked her way through the rest of her routine, bobbling on purpose, making up silly remarks. She was supposed to pull on a rope in the Strong Man's Secret, but she jumped with it instead—and tripped. She got her puppet, Al the Alligator, stuck in his box. As she bumbled along, she could see the students doing exactly what she had dreamed of—sitting up straight and watching her every move. Even Woody was wearing a grin.

But Jo didn't care. She felt as if she were two people, one clowning her way through a silly routine, the other aching to leave the building, to leave the town, to run and run and never come back. When she was through, she stomped offstage with a fake stumble, and scarcely heard the burst of applause.

"They liked us after all," Kim shrilled as they waited backstage for the student aides to carry off their gear.

"Liked *us*! Big help you were!" Jo replied, clenching her teeth. "Running off and leaving me out there alone!"

"Oh, Jo—I just got *scared*." Kim's face was almost as pink as her skirt. "Anyway, you fixed it up okay. It was really great."

"You know it was nothing like what we planned."

"The kids thought it was a blast," Kim insisted. "Listen to them! That's the most they've clapped for anybody!"

"But it wasn't right."

Jo only half listened to the announcement of the next act. As long as she lived, she'd never forget those awful minutes when she'd stood there frozen, not knowing what to do, while the audience rocked and roared.

Instead of being a tall, mystifying, deep-voiced magician, she'd been a clown, and ruined it all. She could never hold her head up again, or face the Merlins, or Woody, or Mr. Paisley. Especially Mr. Paisley. He'd counted on her, and as far as she was concerned, she had let him down.

* Not the Way Jo Planned It

JO AND KIM HURRIEDLY STUFFED THEIR EQUIP-
ment into the suitcase and box and carried them
to the school cafeteria, where other contestants
were waiting.

"Anyway, we finished the act!" Kim said. "I almost
quit, though."

"May we both should have," Jo darkly replied, as
she laid the suitcase on a vacant table, took everything out, and started to repack it with care.

As she worked, she brooded. She'd been rattled,
that's what started it, and then she'd panicked as
if she were about four years old. And she knew
why! She hadn't had the right tricks. Kim hadn't

25

given her the equipment quickly enough. Mr. Paisley had made her use the same old stuff. She was pretty good at Multiplying Billiard Balls. Why hadn't Woody told her to use that?

"Yuk-k-k!" Jo slid the Unbeatable Drum into its box. Try to be fair, she stormed at herself. *She* was the one who had failed. Not her tricks. Not Kim. Or Woody. Or Mr. Paisley. At the first hint of trouble she had turned into an absolute weakfish, and laying it on someone else was the sleaziest, weaseliest thing she could possibly do. She had lost this tryout, but next time she would win. She. Herself. On her own.

When all their gear was properly repacked, Kim went into the hall to hear the other acts, but Jo stayed behind, resting her chin on her fist. In a few minutes one of her classmates, Maria Crawford, dropped down on the bench beside her.

"You were super! I was in the hall, and heard every word!" exclaimed Maria, who was going to sing a solo. "How do you think of such *funny* things?"

"Thanks ... but it wasn't ... exactly ... what I planned." Jo looked up and tried to smile. "Anyway, I hope you win a place, Maria. You have a good chance."

"Not as good as yours. But I'll try. Is it scary, out there on the stage?"

"Sort of. But I'm sure you'll do well."

The two girls wandered on together. They stopped beside Rhonda Moore, a member of the Merlins, who was brushing her black-and-white dog, Rikki. "Hi, Rikki! Have you practiced a lot of tricks?" Jo asked, trying to sound interested.

"Eleven. He's smart," Rhonda replied, while the dog gazed adoringly at her and thumped his tail on the floor.

"Dog-genius. I hope it goes okay." Jo scratched him behind his ears. Dogs were lucky, she thought. They didn't have to worry about judges and tryouts and ruining their acts.

Jo and Maria wished good luck to a member of their science class, who had worked up a skit. They helped a dancer hook up her costume, held a guitar while its owner looked for a missing pick, and talked with a boy who had been silently blowing air through his clarinet.

Later, Jo stood in line with Kim for cookies and hot cocoa, and when the tryout was finished, she forced herself to walk calmly to the back of the auditorium with the other performers.

"I wish I could put my hands over my ears," she whispered to Kim when a tall, square-shouldered man came onstage, carrying a white envelope. "Anyway, it'll soon be over."

The man was Steven Van Horn, the mayor of Madrona, and his voice seemed to drone on forever, dripping long words about the splendid audience and the judges' difficulty in making a choice.

"Hurry up! Give us the bad news," Jo muttered, which sent Kim into a paroxysm of shaky giggles.

At last, when Jo had decided that in one more minute she would explode, Mr. Van Horn opened the envelope. "And now—our winners." The paper crackled in his hand. "Fred Gustofson. For his humorous skit."

A few people clapped, at which the mayor smiled and waved. "Later, if you please. Let's reserve our applause until the end."

The house quieted, and he went on. "Maria Crawford, singing 'Climb Every Mountain.'"

Another spatter of applause, quickly hushed.

"And one more—Joanna Rodgers, for her comedy act, assisted by Kim Eberly. Congratulations to all of you." He slipped the paper into his pocket as the applause began again.

Although the other contestants gathered around Jo, chattering and patting her back, she hardly heard what they said. After falling flat on her face, after doing positively the worst act of her entire life, she had won! But she had done it as a comic, not a real magician. Joanna of the Black Cloak—nuts! She was Joanna the Jerk!

Kim giggled and grabbed Jo's arm. "We *did* it! We're going to the in the big show!"

"Looks like it." Jo managed to keep her voice down. Let Kim twitter as much as she wanted to, but for herself . . . She took a deep breath and put on a goony grin again, the one she'd been wearing for what seemed like forever. *Laugh, clown, laugh!* Okay. She'd do her howling later, when she was alone.

Her brother, Woody, suddenly sauntered up on his long legs, to grin and thump her on the back. "Good going," he said, with a thumbs-up sign.

"Woody . . ." Jo started to make a joke, but gave it up. With him, at least, she could be honest. "Come off it. You know it wasn't right."

"Mmm. It wasn't that bad. Different, maybe. Surprised me"

"It was a mess!"

"Well—not really. You sure saved your skin." He glanced over his shoulder. "Hey, I've got to run. Going to meet a guy." After giving her one more whack, he strode away.

Kim began to talk again, rattling full-speed ahead. "You can think of a lot more comical routines, I know you can. Maybe flowers that won't bloom, or a bird that won't fly. We've got a whole week to practice, and we'll work it out together. We'll . . ."

She stopped, because several more students approached, and then Mrs. Forbes fluttered down the line, out of breath as usual, and teetering along on black, shiny, high-heeled shoes. "Jo! I closed the shop to come—I knew your mother and daddy wouldn't care—and I'm so *glad* I did! I was *so proud*!" She brushed back a stray lock of tightly curled gray hair.

"Why, thank you, Mrs. Forbes." Jo's voice sounded strange, as if it were far away.

"Channel six had a magic act, just last month, and it wasn't a bit better than yours. You didn't have a dull moment. Not one."

Not a dull moment? Jo thought. No, more like a torture chamber. But she tried to sound light. "And I didn't do even one commercial!"

Mrs. Forbes didn't catch the joke—she seldom did. "Really, I feel as if I'd been *living* in a premiere," she whispered. "It was so exciting. But now I've got to hurry back to the shop. I'm cleaning the souvenir shelf, and you know how full that is. I want to keep everything absolutely *immaculate* while I'm there alone. It saves time in the long run." With a final pat of her hand, she trudged toward the door.

After that, students and parents gathered, while Jo pretended to be happy.

Another teacher came past, while Jo pretended to be pleased.

Sidney Larrance had apparently closed his kite shop, because he ambled up, stroking his droopy mustache. "Splendid!" he exclaimed. "A triumph of ingenuity! Our bird flew high today."

"Why, thank you, Sidney," Jo replied. "I'm glad you could come." But as he sauntered away, she wondered. Triumph of ingenuity! Was it praise— or a slap?

And then Mr. Paisley came toward her with hands outstretched and a misty look in his faded blue eyes. "You astonished us all, Joanna."

"Including myself," Jo murmured.

He nodded, gripping her fingers in his cool, dry ones. "This ... this problem ... could happen to anyone, and you handled it like an old-timer. Thinking onstage—that's not easy. I was proud of you."

"For being a funny-face ...?" Jo began, and stopped. She'd been putting on an act with almost everyone, but she couldn't keep it up, not with Mr. Paisley. "I wanted to ... to ..." Although she longed to explain, her homeroom teacher interrupted to talk about the all-school show. Then a group of excited Merlins surged in, and by the time they were finished, Mr. Paisley had gone.

"See! I told you everybody liked it!" insisted Kim when they were alone.

"At least it's over. But next week we'll do ..."

"Something funny? Maybe a trick with Bouncing Balls? You're pretty good at juggling. Or ..."

"Something special." Jo didn't explain; she couldn't, because she hadn't made a plan, except that it definitely *wouldn't be a joke*! Besides, it was time to go home, and here was Kim's mother, ready to give her a ride.

An hour later, after they had stopped for a hamburger and strawberry milkshake, she lugged her suitcase and box into the kitchen. Woody was there, tall and lanky, standing beside the counter and slathering peanut butter on four slices of bread. "Well! The Great Siegfrieda herself!" he exclaimed. "Sandwich?" Jo had never decided which was more important to Woody, his computer or food.

"Not a bite," she told him, trying to sound casual.

"Milk? Coke?"

"Nope. I'm stuffed."

His eyes were sober. "Jo ..." He hesitated. "You don't have to feel so down. I know it wasn't the way you planned, but the kids liked it. They said ..."

Jo didn't look at him. "Let's skip it," she mumbled.

"Sure. But gosh—changing your whole act like that. It took guts."

"Maybe." If she tried to say another word, she'd absolutely blubber.

"Jo ..." He bit into his sandwich. "If you think buying some new material will help, I'll ... well ... I've got a little dough saved up. I could lend you some, or ..."

"Thanks, Woody." Jo clenched her teeth against a storm of sobs. "That's really great of you. But I don't want to think about it now."

"You don't have to turn so high and mighty. I just ..."

"Woody! I told you ... *I don't want ... to talk about it!* Besides, I've got to put this stuff away." The last words floated after her as she turned and carried her box and suitcase upstairs, stumbling over the top step because everything was blurred by tears.

Jo loved her room, which was large and on a corner, with a long view of the Pacific Ocean from one window and the dark green branches of a fir tree almost touching the other. She had put up posters—Siegfried with a snow leopard; David Copperfield with his magician's cabinet; Houdini in chains. A writing desk stood against the wall, and on it was one of her favorite possessions—an extension telephone, in a glossy finish of midnight blue.

But today she didn't glance at the posters, or pick up a *Conjurer's Digest* from the pile on the window seat, or telephone a friend. Setting the suitcase and box in a corner, she dropped onto the bed and began to pet Duchess, her long-haired cat, who had been asleep there. Duchess rolled over, stretched all four legs, and opened her pink mouth in a yawn, while Jo curled her fingers in the soft fur. "At least you aren't blathering about how super it was," she whispered.

Here, with only Duchess to see her, she could wipe off the gooey grin and stop trying to pretend that everything was all right. She could blubber as hard as she wanted to, and call herself a hundred names, and pound the pillow with both fists. Duchess would never tell.

In the Rolltop Desk

WHEN JO CAME DOWNSTAIRS THE NEXT MORN-
ing, Mrs. Forbes was at the kitchen table, delicately
sipping coffee while she watched the news on her
roll-around TV. She was dressed for the shop, in a
blue skirt and ruffled blouse, with a silver brooch
at her throat. "That sounds like Jo," she said, without turning her head. "You've beaten Woody today.
He's still asleep."

"He worked late on his computer game." Jo
poured a glass of orange juice and filled a bowl
with cereal. "He and Paul Aiken are inventing one."

"Magic! Computers! Inventing a game! What you
young folks won't do!" Mrs. Forbes clucked her

tongue, still watching the screen. "No rain in sight, at least for a couple of days."

At the next commercial she turned toward Jo. "Cold cereal? Is that all you're having? Young folks need lots of food, to build them up. Wouldn't you like some eggs? Or I could make pancakes."

Jo gulped. She had tried Mrs. Forbes's leathery pancakes once, and once was enough. "Oh, this is fine. I'm in a hurry," she hastily said.

"You're not starting the morning right. I believe that a good breakfast means a good day. But if your mother doesn't care ..." Mrs. Forbes turned back to the television. "Another robbery! I don't know what this world is coming to. Anyhow, it's almost time for me to leave. Now let's see—which of you is coming to the shop today?"

"I am, and I won't forget," Jo promised, for she and Woody were taking turns as helper in the Jolly Rodgers. "I'll be there by one."

"It does seem too bad, taking up your time," said Mrs. Forbes, her forehead puckered with worry. "Young folks ought to have spring vacation entirely free. I might ..."

"Please! It's *all right*," Jo interrupted. If only Mrs. Forbes wouldn't try so hard! "We don't mind a bit! Running the shop plus the house, all alone, would be too hard for you."

"I suppose. Anyway, your parents said you were to help." Mrs. Forbes clucked her tongue again, and a few minutes later she cautiously shepherded the family station wagon out of the drive.

With tousled hair hanging over his forehead, Woody soon clumped into the room; and just as he finished breakfast, his friend Paul came to work on their game. Jo, who was making a stack of tuna sandwiches, could hear excited shouts. "Quick!" "Give it the stick!"

They called her in to try it out, but she didn't stay long. Instead, she left most of the sandwiches for the boys, put her own lunch into her backpack, picked up her wallet, which held her baby-sitting money, and wheeled her bicycle out of the garage.

Their house was a large one in the new part of town, high on the hills, and Jo loved this view of Madrona Bay and the rocky inlet that connected it to the Pacific Ocean—blue today, with a silvery shine far out to sea. But she gave it only a quick glance, then caught a deep breath of the brisk ocean air and started out.

She coasted downhill into Old Town, beside the bay. Solemn gray and white seagulls sat on the pilings. A wooden building had a sign in its window; "We buy fern, salal, huckleberry, laurel, cascara bark." Enormous nets were strewn on a weedy storage lot, orange crab pots stood in stacks higher than her head, and rope as thick as a wrist lay in coils. Passing these, passing the gabled shops, Jo soon reached the Cave.

"Are you here?" she asked as she walked in. The room was dim and dusty, as if it hadn't been disturbed for years.

"He's coming, no doubt, he's coming. But he isn't open yet," Sidney's mocking voice replied, and he waved to her from his end of the hallway. "Ah-ha! Our young prestidigitator! Greetings! My humble abode will shelter you, and my time is yours." With a sweeping bow he motioned her into his half of the building.

To Jo, the inside of Sky High seemed like the middle of a kaleidoscope. Red and yellow, blue and purple and green kites—the ones with dragons and snowflakes, bat wings and stars—hung on the walls, their long tails draped in loops. Below them, bunches of wind socks dangled from circles of steel, like racks of clothes in a department store, filling the room.

Jo threaded her way between the clumps—yellow daffodils, black and white cows wearing red bows, fish with glittery scales, a patchwork cat with its pink tongue hanging out. Sidney was half-hidden among the streamers, but she followed along until they emerged into his work area at the back, where he not only sold kites but designed and made them, extra-fine ones, Jo thought. "I hope Mr. Paisley opens soon," she said. "I need a new trick in a hurry."

"Hmm! We all crave instant solutions!" Sidney

stopped beside his worktable, which held swirls of bright-colored Mylar and sailcloth and taffeta. "We sustain ourselves on hope eternal, but perfection dangles just beyond our ken. As you and I are unhappily aware." He arched his eyebrows and winked.

"I guess," Jo replied with a giggle. She wasn't always sure what Sidney meant, but he could be fun.

"Speaking of hope ..." He picked up a half-finished kite shaped like multicolored stars within stars. "A supernova—my entry for the Festival of Kites, up in Mitchell. It better be good. Competition is fierce, and I need the cash."

"It's beautiful! And so big!" Jo exclaimed.

"Yeah. Actually a bit oversize." Grinning, he held it above his head. "But I don't think the judges will measure them, so I'm risking exposure for the sake of the extra lift."

"You're going to enter it? As a high flyer?"

"Sure. Nobody'll notice." Sidney guided it through a gentle swoop, while Jo watched, feeling troubled. Only a few weeks ago he had shown her half a dozen kites made of bargain Mylar, and when she'd asked him whether they were durable, he had only shrugged and said it didn't matter; that the Mylar would save him a bundle, and if the kites broke, he'd make another sale. Sidney was amusing, but she wished he wouldn't cheat.

"It ought to top everything else there," he said, as he perched on the edge of the table. "But getting back to you, Jo—you need a new trick? I thought you had at least a couple dozen."

"Maybe. I've a lot, anyway. But I'm in an awful mess!"

"A mess! What kind of mess could a kid like you get into?" Sidney jerked his head toward the colorful jumble. "Me, now. Look at that conglomeration! And it isn't half paid for! Ravenous creditors are yammering at my heels—in spite of my bargain Mylar." He winked at her. "While you ... Young. Smart. Talented magician. Just wowed them in your first big show."

Jo looked at the floor.

"So ... it wasn't quite what you had in mind?"

"Not ... not exactly." Jo didn't want to talk about it, not even with Sidney, and she was relieved to hear the jingle of the Cave's doorbell. "There's Mr. Paisley! I'll go now!" she exclaimed, and ran through the clusters of wind socks, down the hallway, and into the Cave.

"I'm *so* glad you're back!" she gasped. "I've been waiting."

Mr. Paisely was in the rear corner, starting a fire in the stove, but he stood up at once and shuffled foward to meet her. "Joanna! I was hoping you'd come. Again, congratulations!"

"Congratulations? Oh, Mr. Paisley, no! I flopped."

"Flopped? No, Joanna. I was there, and saw you pull yourself together like a seasoned performer. That was no flop."

Jo looked at the wide, dark boards of the floor with black steaks between them. "The people laughed."

"Yes. And it hurt."

He sounded so gentle that the hard knot inside Jo started to untangle. Slowly at first, then in a torrent of words, she told him how disgraced she felt. "I tried, I really tried, to do it right," she finished. "My mom and dad helped me, and so did Woody. And then ..." She seemed to hear the guffaws again, and Mr. Van Horn's announcement. "It was gruesome. He called me a *comic*!"

"I understand. But truly, Joanna. Is that so bad?"

Jo drew a deep breath. "Yes! It was *awful*! I know lots of magicians do comic acts, but they intend to, and mine was just an accident. It wasn't *me,* at all. I want to be real, not funny. Mr. Paisley, please find me the very best trick you have."

"A new device?" He shook his head.

"Please? I *really* want one."

Mr. Paisley sighed. "You think it will help? Well, let's see.... how about the Flying Ace? No, too small." He started along the shelves. "The Dove in a Cage? It's excellent, but expensive. How much can you spare?"

"Quite a lot. I've been saving up for a new bike,

but I'd rather spend it on this," Jo replied, and watched him slide the Dove out of its box.

For the next half hour she and Mr. Paisley searched for the perfect trick, but everything they found was too small, or confusing, or almost like something she already had. They were interrupted several times by the jingle of the shop bell. Some of the customers had plenty of money, others had only a little; some were young, in jeans and T-shirts; one was a white-haired woman who bought a beginner's set. "For my grandson," she explained.

When she was gone, Mr. Paisley began to rummage along the shelves once more, blowing off an occasional puff of dust. "Magnetic Balls? They're difficult, but effective. Do you want to try them?" He handed her a dark green box with a picture of silver balls.

Jo shook her head. "Mr. Paisley—couldn't we please have a look out there?" She pointed toward the door that led to the back room. "I'd like something really professional."

Mr. Paisley frowned.

"Even if it's hard. I'll practice it every day."

His frown deepened. "Joanna, you're pursuing a will-o'-the-wisp. It's you yourself that counts. Not what you find in a box."

"Please?"

"I keep my most valuable materials there. I never allow ..." Pulling his glasses down his nose, he looked at her over their tops. "But you want it so much ..."

"If I could just look. Maybe ..."

Mr. Paisley sighed. "I understand. You won't be satisfied until you've checked it for yourself. So ..."

She didn't dare move.

"We'll try." Mr. Paisley fished in his pocket for his keys.

The hinges squeaked as he opened the narrow door, and a draft of cold air brushed across Jo's cheeks. She hesitated. The room was so big! A vault! An abyss! But she wanted to see it, and now she had a chance, so she drew a deep breath and walked down three worn wooden steps.

She stopped at the bottom to sniff the faint odor of fish and dust and old wood. She glanced up at the ceiling, bare and high, and at the four small windows almost touching it, with ragged cobwebs fluttering across their corners. Outside, a gull screamed, and the splash of waves from a passing boat made the dark floor quiver.

"So, what do you think of it?" Mr. Paisley asked with a wry smile. "Perhaps you were expecting something grand? Or warm? The heat from my stove doesn't reach this far." He folded his arms and tucked his hands under his coat sleeves.

"It's big," Jo replied in a whisper. "But there isn't ... very much in it." Except for a clutter of old furniture, the room was almost empty.

Mr. Paisley led her toward the side, where shelves held an assortment of large boxes. "If you find a treasure, it will be here, among my professional materials. However, they require considerable skill."

Jo timidly touched a carton labeled LEVITATOR. "Is this what they use to raise people up?"

"That's right. But, Joanna, it's out of your range, both in price and ability." Mr. Paisley lifted down another. "Now here—the Conjurer's Snake. It takes clever handling, but you could master it if you work hard. Can you get things out of your coattails pretty well?"

"I think we'd better look at something else." Jo liked the secret pockets in the coattails of her magician's cloak, but she remembered how Woody had laughed when she tried to use them and made them flap.

Walking to the next shelf, Mr. Paisley opened another box. "The Chameleon Clubs. You were doing quite well as a juggler, the last I knew. How is it now?"

"I've been practicing, and I like it." Jo hesitantly picked up one of the clubs, silver-colored and heavy. "They're pretty, all right, but they're so big. And in a show ..."

"You'll be wise not to try," he agreed. "Only fools attempt tricks beyond their skill."

Jo laid her hand on a large blue box with a picture

of a girl on its cover. "This—the Changing Chest?"

Mr. Paisley shook his head. "It's a fine one, no doubt of that. Its operator puts a girl into the glass cubicle, drapes it, and removes the drape to find a different girl. But it's too complicated for you, or for your rosy-cheeked little assistant. She couldn't do it, even if you could. It would frighten her."

"This platform?"

"Essentially the same."

They looked at a cabinet in which a person could be sawed in half and a seemingly solid trunk from which the operator could escape. They were too difficult.

They looked at candles that were to be fastened to the fingers and lighted. "They'll never allow it, on a school stage," Mr. Paisley said, and Jo knew that was so.

They moved toward the jumble of furniture—a table loaded with smaller boxes of tricks, two bookcases, a settee with green velvet cushions, several chairs, and a battered, dark rolltop desk. "You've heard of this, I'm sure. It's my Capricorn section. Actually my elephant—a white one." He smiled at his own joke.

Jo knew that Mr. Paisley's beginner's table was chiefly supplied with what he called "Capricorn tricks," but she didn't know exactly what they were or where they were from. "How did you get your Capricon things?" she asked, feeling curious.

"Capricorn?" He stopped beside the table. "It was a small shop near the California border—shabby and poorly equipped—owned by a fellow named Henry Blake. Last fall, after Blake died, a fellow at the Magicians' Convention told me the stock was for sale, and cheap. I'd heard about it, of course. Most magicians had, at least here on the West Coast." He was fumbling with the objects on the table, picking them up, glancing into the boxes, setting them down again. "We knew Henry's shop wasn't good for much, and wondered how he made ends meet; and we'd heard that Henry was an ingenious fellow, always mixed up in a new scheme. But he was a bit—standoffish."

"Even with magicians?" asked Jo.

"With everyone, as far as we could tell. Rumor had it that he'd devised a mysterious plan for making a fortune, and that he'd once been in prison. And then, after he died . . ." He paused.

"Was he sick?"

"Heart attack—sudden." Mr. Paisley's faded blue eyes were vague behind the gold-rimmed glasses. "Anyway, when I learned that Henry's stock was for sale, I went to see it, and bought it out, lock, stock, and barrel." He patted a green velvet sofa, setting up a cloud of dust. "Look at these all you wish, but they won't help you. This summer, when the tourists come, I'm going to sell them off, at bargain prices."

He started toward another shelf, just as the shop bell jingled. "Hello?" he called, looking toward the narrow door. "Hello?"

"Paisley?" came a muffled voice from the front of the shop. "Where are you?"

"On my way," he replied, then added more softly, "Joanna, I'm needed out in front, but I think . . . I'm sure . . . you are responsible. You have good judgment, and if, this summer . . ."

"Yes?"

"I'm sure I can trust you." Mr. Paisley was speaking more firmly now. "So you may stay and search for your heart's desire. If something pleases you, bring it out, and I'll see whether it's suitable." He waved a hand, and shuffled toward the narrow door.

Left alone, Jo hastily inspected the rest of the advanced boxes, but they were so complicated that she soon left them and moved toward the articles from Capricorn. She passed the sofa and some chairs and stopped beside the rolltop desk, which was standing by itself with its cover pulled down as if it had its eyes shut.

Jo wondered how the sliding top worked, and Mr. Paisley had told her she could look around, so she grasped the cover by both handles and gave it a tug. It was tight at first, then jerked free and slid easily with a soft, rubbing sound. Inside she found a flat workspace and several rows of cubbyholes, which were marked: "Bills." "Receipts." "Stock." "Stamps."

Seeing nothing in them, she looked next at the drawers, four down each side, and a wide one in the center. Not expecting to find anything, merely curious, she pulled out the middle one. Empty. So was the top one on the right, and the one just below. Drawer by drawer, she went through them all, giving each a sharp tug, because they were tight.

The last one she tried was at the bottom on the left, and it surprised her by coming all the way out with a rush. She dropped it, picked it up to replace it—and it seemed too short! Surely the others weren't shaped like that! Spreading her fingers as wide as she could, she used them as a crude measuring stick—and yes, this drawer was different.

That's funny! thought Jo. An empty desk, with one short drawer. Could it have a hidden place behind it, like the ones she'd read about? *Of course not!* She almost said it aloud. Secret compartments existed in books, not in Mr. Paisley's desk! But just to make sure, she bent down and peered into the opening where the drawer had been, and even in the dim light she could see that the space was unusually small.

Could there be a secret drawer after all? Could it have a lever to press? If so ...

The end of the slot was closed off by a smooth partition, too far back for Jo's fingers to reach, so she took a pencil out of her backpack and poked with the eraser. Nothing happened. She moved it an inch, poked again—and again—until she heard a click, and the entire rear segment slid forward as if a spring had been released. It couldn't be true— but it was! A secret drawer!

Jo's heart was pounding as she pulled it farther out and found that it contained a brown, stiff, leather box, tooled all over with what looked like stars and comets. It had one word in large letters, angling across the top: TRANSMUTER.

"Transmuter." Jo said it aloud. What did that mean? A change? To go someplace? It didn't matter. This thing was so special that somebody had hidden it in a secret drawer. Sitting down right where she was, on the dusty floor, she unsnapped the leather cover.

Inside was a folded shawl, glowing with color and soft as a handful of down. Next was a gray box, about the size of a small calculator, with a row of colored buttons along the middle. And last of all was a folded paper, stiff and crackling, which Jo spread out on her lap. Most of it was covered with tiny scribbles in purple ink, which seemed to be foreign words, or little pictures—perhaps Chinese. But away down at the bottom were two lists of colors written in English, and a warning. "Destroyed by heat. Disintegrates at temperatures above 110°."

As Jo read them, her heart began to thump. This thing must have been stowed away by Henry Blake of the mysterious plans. He was an inventor. A magician. This might be worthless—or it might be a superwonderful magic device. She liked the crackly feel of the paper, the softness and color of the shawl, and the squiggly scribbles. Her fingers itched to experiment with those colored buttons, and the more she turned it over in her hands, the more she wanted it for her own. A trick, a joke, a guide to hidden treasure—whatever it might be, she had to try it out.

Should she show it to Mr. Paisley, and ask him to sell it to her?

"NO!" She said it aloud. He'd said all his best tricks were too hard and expensive, and told her to find something sensible. He might say that about TRANSMUTER, too, and she'd have to put it back.

But if she bought it casually, as if it were a plain, common Capricorn trick . . .

Deceive him? Mr. Paisley? she asked herself. That wouldn't be fair!

It isn't valuable, something inside her replied. *Nothing from Capricorn is. Mr. Paisley said so himself. He won't care.*

It's cheating! He's your friend!

Mr. Paisley won't know the difference. He doesn't even know it's here! Why not . . . why not . . . Yes! Why not take it home, and figure it out, and give him a surprise! Jo's breath came fast as she carefully returned everything to the leather box, replaced the desk drawers, and bounded into the front part of the Cave.

After the chill of the back room, the warmth felt

wonderful, for the fire was bright now, and Jo waited beside the stove until Mr. Paisley's customer had gone. "So, what have you found?" he asked then. "Something good, I hope."

"I think so. See?" As nonchalantly as possible, she gave him the trick.

"Transmuter!" he read. "I don't recall anything of that name. Where was it?"

"In the old desk." She didn't mention the secret drawer.

"Hmm. Capricorn stuff." Mr. Paisley rubbed his forehead, looking at her with a puzzled frown. "I thought ... I was almost sure I had checked the entire shipment when it came in, and I didn't see ... In the desk, you say?"

"That's right," Jo faltered.

"I must have forgotten." Rubbing his forehead, he looked at her for a long moment, then lifted the leather cover and inspected the items, one by one. "Are you sure this is what you want? Joanna, I'm afraid that nothing from Capricorn will offer you a challenge."

"I'm sure," Jo insisted. "It's so different. So—peculiar."

"Yes. Very." Mr. Paisley flipped his fingers over the colored buttons. "Transmuter. It looks like a simple vanisher," he continued, using the magicians' term for a device that makes things seem to disappear.

Jo didn't move.

"The usual concealing shawl," he continued. "Joanna, objects of this type are manufactured by the score. They look impressive—even this one has quite a nice shawl. But they're very difficult to use."

"Anyway, I'd like to try it, and see."

"Joanna, believe me, this is worthless." Mr. Paisley looked at her with a puzzled frown. "What intrigues you so?"

She touched the shawl. "Just . . . I just *want* it. It's . . . well, it's interesting."

"And flimsy. It won't help you. It'll take up your time, when you ought to be working on your act."

"I'll work on my act, truly I will. But I want this, too. I *like* it." Jo opened her mouth to tell him about the exciting secret drawer, but closed it at once.

Mr. Paisley shook his head and started to refold the shawl, and just as he replaced it in the leather box, the shop bell tinkled again. "In one minute," he called out, as he hastily closed the box and snapped its cover. "I think you're making a mistake," he added to Jo. "But if it's what you want . . . The price?"

"Isn't it marked?"

Mr. Paisley turned the leather box over, looking at all sides. "No mark. And there's no use checking the stock list, because I haven't recorded any Capricorn material. Not worth it." He glanced uneasily toward the customer who had come in and was fiddling with the items on a table. "Let's just call it a gift."

"Oh, no, Mr. Paisley! You gave me a present Saturday. I want to buy this one."

"My independent Miss Joanna!" His face softened in a smile. "All right. For five dollars, I will sell it to you; but I'm afraid you've made a poor choice."

"I don't care. I want it." Jo drew a bill out of her wallet, and a moment later, while Mr. Paisley shuffled toward his customer, she tucked TRANSMUTER —her TRANSMUTER now—into her backpack.

Just as she turned to leave, she heard steps in the hallway, and Sidney shambled in. "Oh—sorry! Thought I heard the bell," he said, stroking his mustache. But when he noticed that the narrow door was still open, he seemed to freeze in place. "Hey, friend Paisley, you really ought to watch this! Problems, you know! Can't be too careful!" After fishing in his pocket for a large bunch of keys, he closed the door and locked it, then glanced at Jo through narrowed eyes and stomped back up the hall.

Jo paid him little attention. She had her trick— cryptic and exciting—and she couldn't wait to try it out. In an hour she must be at the Jolly Rodgers to help Mrs. Forbes. Since she couldn't ride home and back in an hour, she'd ride down to the city park instead, and look over her purchase. Down there beside the bay, where she could be alone, she'd find out what TRANSMUTER could do.

The Colors of the Rainbow

A BRIGHT SUN WAS SHINING ON THE PEAKED roofs as Jo pedaled swiftly down Old Main Street toward the Neck, which was a narrow, rocky inlet leading from Madrona Bay to the Pacific Ocean. The highway bridge across it loomed ahead of her, a soaring arch, high overhead. It was pure, serene, white against the blue sky.

Around the bridge supports and all along the shore of the Neck was the city park where Jo had learned magic in Mr. Paisley's summer class, and here she stopped to sit down on a moss-covered log. The park was cool, shaded by fir trees that rustled overhead in the stiff ocean breeze. Shrubs of wild rhododendron bore lavish pink clusters of bloom, and the tide was rushing in like a river. Jo was alone now, and could examine TRANSUMUTER.

However, just as she started to take it out of her backpack, Rhonda Moore came jogging along the path with her dog, Rikki. "Jo!" She made a sudden stop. "The Merlins are really proud of you! That was a good act."

"I thought it was a flop," Jo mumbled as she petted Rikki, who had sat down and was thumping his tail on the ground. "Good dog! I wish he could be in the show. The audience really liked him."

Rhonda shrugged. "Maybe next year. I'm going to teach him a lot of new tricks. Look." When she waved her hand in a circle, he rolled over. "How about you? Are you ready for Friday?"

"Well—I have an idea. But I don't know how well it will work."

While they were talking, two of Woody's friends glided past on skateboards and whirled to a stop. "Hey—there's Jo!" the taller one shouted. "That was some trick, that one with the fan. How'd you do it, anyway?"

"Magic, of course!" How wonderful! He hadn't called her act a joke. "You don't really think I'd tell my secrets, do you?"

"I guess not." The boy grinned back. "That is, if you were doing real magic. But a clown act is ..."

"Clown!" Jo felt like a punctured balloon. "Listen! I know I acted like a fool, but I can do regular magic tricks, too. Wait till Friday. You'll see."

"I'll be there."

Rhonda picked up a stick and tossed it up the knoll. "Fetch, Rikki!" she called, and the dog took off with a scruffle of fir needles.

"Hey! He's *fast*!" exclaimed the other boy, a stocky one, with a high-pitched voice. "Let's have a game."

Although Jo laughed with them and tried her hand at tossing the stick, she was fuming inside. Was that all they remembered—that her act was funny? They didn't have any idea, not the faintest, of what she wanted to do! They didn't even know what real magic was! *Why didn't they leave*? She'd *perish* if she couldn't get into that leather box!

Minute after minute slipped away, and by the time the boys scooted off, Jo's free hour was nearly gone. "I've got to rush! It's my day at the shop!" she exclaimed, after a frantic glance at her watch. "Woody and I take turns helping Mrs. Forbes."

"How gruesome," Rhonda said. "Spring vacation, too."

"Oh, I don't mind. Forbesy's all right." But I *do* mind, today, Jo grumbled to herself as she mounted her bicycle and started back to town with the leather box in her backpack, still unopened.

The Jolly Rodgers, specializing in high-quality brass, was near the far end of Old Main Street, in a tall, square building with a pointed arch over the front door. Jo rode into its rear lot, pushed her bicycle up the steps into the storeroom, and carefully laid her backpack on a small table, hidden by her jacket. "I'm here!" she called, as she went into the front.

Mrs. Forbes was there alone, a lock of hair straggling across her forehead as she vigorously dusted a display of small souvenirs—unicorn letter openers, duck bookends, bells, planters, and key chains. A portable radio stood nearby, with a man droning on about coastal gardens and compost heaps.

"Jo, this is nice of you." Mrs. Forbes turned down the volume. "I wouldn't let you spend your precious vacation this way, but your mother made the plan, and ..."

"It's all right. I don't mind." Another fib! Jo told herself. She minded a whole lot. "Mrs. Forbes," she added aloud, "Mom and Dad don't expect you to do all this cleaning. Just keep the shop open."

"Yes, but there's a lot to think about. These new lamps, now. I think your parents would want them featured. Shall I put them on the shelf with the bowls?"

"That sounds fine," Jo said.

"It will mean moving the clocks again, but we can do that easily enough," Mrs. Forbes continued.

"I want it to look nice when they come back."

Jo smiled. "It will. They love this place. Anyway, I'll give you a hand." After unpacking the lamps, she helped Mrs. Forbes move all the clocks to a lower shelf and started to dust her favorite piece, a brass cargo light from England.

Before she had finished that, the door opened, admitting a customer, and for the rest of the afternoon Jo alternately cleaned the stock and waited on shoppers. She sold a brass walrus, a large tray, a wall plaque of metallic pine boughs, and a bell. But eventually, when she thought she couldn't wait another minute, it was time to load the bicycle into the family station wagon and drive up the long hill. As soon as they reached the house, Woody came clattering down the stairs. "Hi, Jo. Kim telephoned. I said you'd call her back."

"Okay. After dinner." Jo paused on the bottom step.

"Find anything in the Cave?"

"Maybe. I'm not sure."

"Well, good luck." Woody gave her arm a friendly poke as he ambled toward the back of the house to take his turn at helping Mrs. Forbes with the meal.

Upstairs in her own silver and blue room, Jo flung her jacket onto a chair, gave Duchess a quick pat, and shoved the stuffed animals aside. Sitting on the edge of her bed, close to the desk, she unsnapped her backpack. At last—at last—after all this time, she could see what TRANSMUTER was really like!

She started by examining the leather case, which was stiff, square-cornered, and elaborately decorated with raised designs of stars and comets, planets with rings like Saturn, and cresent moons. As she remembered, its cover had one word, TRANSMUTER, interlaced with strange-looking flowers on thorny stems. She'd look up that word and find out exactly what it meant; but first she would try to work the trick.

Cautiously she lifted the hinged lid, and there was the shawl, faintly fragrant, neatly folded and lying on top. When she shook it out, she found it was patterned in swirls of red and blue, purple and green and gold, vivid as sunshine through a stained-glass window. It was fringed, large, and strangely lightweight, lying like gossamer across her arm. She draped it over the back of a chair, where it hung in clinging folds; and although she half expected the chair to collapse, nothing happened. No lightning flashes, no mysterious taps, not even a quiver. Drawing a deep breath of the shawl's exotic scent, she refolded it into its original small square and laid it on top of the math book on her desk.

The next object in the leather case was the gray box, not quite as large as a paperback book and heavier than she had realized—heavier than a rock of similar size—heavier than any small thing she had ever lifted. Except for that, it reminded her of a cassette player, with a row of buttons along the center, unlabeled, and each of a different color.

The only remaining item was the paper, which Jo carefully unfolded and carried to the window, where the light was better. There they were—the purple squiggles and foreign words, the English list of colors, and the warning she had read before. "Destroyed by heat. Disintegrates at temperatures above 110°."

What was it, anyway? Would it explode? Bewildered, a little frightened, Jo left the window, sat down again on the edge of the bed, and ran her finger down the list. Of course! she realized at once. They were the colors of the rainbow, just as she had learned them in art class.

The button at the left end was violet, and violet was mentioned in the list. Next was a rather dark blue-violet shade, probably the one the list called indigo—another rainbow word. The rest were easy, and when Jo had checked them all, she pressed them in order, left to right. Violet. Indigo. Blue. Green. Yellow. Orange. Red. They went down silently but with a slight resistance, as if they were on springs. And at the end was one more color, not of the rainbow. Black.

Jo studied the printed sheet again. The first list was short, saying only, "Green. Yellow. Red.

Orange. Yellow. Red. Red. Three seconds. Black."

"Does that sound like anything to you?" she asked Duchess, who opened one eye and yawned. After reading the paper again, but still finding no explanation, Jo decided to take a chance, press the buttons in the order they were given on the list, and see what happened.

With the leather case still in her lap, the folded shawl on top of the math book, and the box in one hand, she started. Green. She pressed it. Yellow. Next to the green one. Red. She followed them carefully, saying each one under her breath. How dull it was! No blinking lights, not even a beep!

She read the directions once more. "Three seconds. Black." Did that mean to hurry and finish it in three seconds, or to wait that long? She'd already waited three seconds—longer, in fact—so she'd go ahead. Black!

She gave it a firm press. Nothing happened. She was just sitting quietly on the edge of the bed, and she'd felt nothing, heard nothing, except . . . Where was the shawl?

Her scalp prickled as she jumped to her feet, letting the leather case slide off her lap with a thud. "Hey!" she shouted. The shawl was gone! So was the math book! But they ought to be right there on the desk! Almost afraid, she reached out, drew back her hand, reached further, and yes—she could feel them both, the shawl still folded in a soft square,

the book still closed. She lifted its invisible cover—
and easily found the corner she had turned down
to mark her place. She riffled the pages she couldn't
see—and they made the same soft whirr that pages
always did. It must be her math book, but it was
as invisible as a piece of glass, so clear she could
see the desk, with its wavy brown grain, right
through the place where the book must be.

Jo's hands trembled as she flipped through the
pages again. This was a vanisher all right, just as
Mr. Paisley had said, and it was *tremendous!* What
an act she could put on now! Bright-colored images
floated into her mind of things that could disappear
onstage. A blackboard. A birdcage. *The piano!* All
she'd hoped for was a special set of cubes that
burst into fantastic shapes, or scarves that stuck
together, or a flying bird—something that would
fool the audience. Instead, she had this!

But what was it, anyway? A plain ordinary vanisher might cover something up, but it couldn't let
you see through it. Could this be real magic? The
kind in fairy stories, with sorcerers and genies in
bottles and ogres and spells? Was there Something
or Somebody in her room right now, towering
above her, with its head as high as the ceiling and
wings outstetched? Ready to fly out the window if
she wanted it to? To take her along with it? There
must be. Nothing else would explain it. Capricorn
had been a peculiar shop—Mr. Paisley had said

so—and that was where TRANSMUTER came from.

She must call Kim right away, so they could plan their act together, the most mind-boggling, stupefying, *earth-shaking* act that had ever been done. They wouldn't tell a soul about it until their *great,* their *unimaginable* thing happened onstage. And she would be up there, in her magician's black cloak, doing it all.

But first she'd have to learn exactly how to use the Trick, which meant getting the book and the shawl back as fast as she could. If Mrs. Forbes came in and touched that invisible book lying on the desk, it would scare her out of her skin.

Dropping down onto the edge of the bed, Jo picked up the direction sheet in hopes that the other list, the long one, would undo the first.

"Violet. Indigo. Blue." The first three buttons on the box. After pressing them, she saw that they were repeated—and again, and still again. The same thing over and over? She reread them, and yes, they were listed four times, so she carefully counted them off, and then came to something different at last. "Green. Yellow. Orange. Blue. Indigo. Red. Yellow. Violet. Indigo." She went through it all. "Wait five seconds. White."

But there wasn't any white key. How could she finish without the right button? Her throat was tight, and her hands were shaking so violently she nearly dropped the box, but she spoke aloud to herself. "Lighten up, Joanna. It's got to be there!" Willing herself to be calm, willing her hands not to slip, she examined the box top, the ends, the sides, and finally turned it over and found the last button underneath.

"White." She pressed the key.

They appeared—the scarf, the book—in their neat little pile on the desk.

TRANSMUTER worked.

What Happened in Jo's Room

JO STARED AT HER MATH BOOK. IT LOOKED THE same as always, gray-blue, stodgy, with crisp, sharp corners and a cover design of interlaced squares. Timidly opening it to the turned-down page, she read problem number five, the one she hadn't figured out yet, and it was still confusing. She lifted a page, and it was white as ever, covered with the usual printing. She made a small tear in it, and it was a common jagged rip, feathered along both edges, like the one she'd made last week when she tried to find her place in a hurry. What had happened? A few minutes ago everything in the book—the paper, the cover, every atom and molecule—

had been changed in some way so it couldn't be seen; but now it was restored, solemn and solid as ever.

Spooky! she thought, glancing at the David Copperfield poster on the wall. Maybe he could explain this, if he were here. But even though she couldn't understand it, she decided to "transmute" something else. She draped the shawl over her reading lamp—and Woody walked past her door, giving it a thump. "Jo! Dinner!"

"Garbage!" How could she leave TRANSMUTER now? But if she didn't, he might come after her; and she didn't want to tell anyone, not even Woody, what had happened until she understood it herself. Carefully replacing the parts of the trick in the leather case, she hid them in the bottom drawer of her chest, under a pile of pajamas.

Just as Jo started down the stairs, Woody came out of his room again, pulling on a blue sweater. "Hey, what's up?" he exclaimed. "You let out a screech, and something banged, and ..."

"Never mind, now. Later." Jo paused on the landing. "I suppose you helped with dinner. What is it?"

Woody clutched his stomach. "One of Forbesy's specials—macaroni and cheese. In other words, flour paste. Only a great talent could do that to perfectly good ingredients." Pretending to groan, he clattered on down the stairs.

In the dining room, Jo did her best to eat; but

the macaroni was thick and dry, so she only poked at it, while her thoughts whirled like one of Sidney's spinning kites.

She'd ask Kim to come over right away, so they could plan how to show off this wonderful trick. They'd use a chair! Kim's table! The microphone! She'd love a new costume, silver and black, but she couldn't manage that, with Mom and Dad away. However, she could wear her mother's highest heels, so she'd be tall and menacing, and spread the sleeves of her coat like bat wings. She'd frown with her eyebrows while she drew her lips into a sinister smile. She'd make her voice sound like a cracked bell. Or a foghorn. Or a chant.

At first she paid little attention to Woody's chatter about his game and Mrs. Forbes's puzzled questions, but when she heard her own name, she came to with a jolt.

Mrs. Forbes, fluttery and pink-cheeked, was looking at her. "And you, Jo—how did you like it?"

"What? Oh—I'm sorry. You said ..."

"Woody's game. I think it's wonderful, the way you young people pick up on the new ideas. For me—I have trouble with the cash register!" Pursing her lips in a self-conscious smile, she poured another cup of tea.

"I told her how great you are," Woody said with a wink.

"Great! Not exactly. I lose every time."

"Don't feel bad. Nobody can make a decent score until we get the bugs out." Woody launched into a long explanation.

A few minutes later Mrs. Forbes turned toward Jo again. "Did you and Kim have a chance to practice this morning?"

She already asked me that, at the store, Jo thought, but she cautiously replied, "Not today. I think we will this evening."

"So late?" Mrs. Forbes's smile faded to a worried frown. "Does your mother let you do that?"

"She doesn't care."

"Well, I suppose it's all right then. Be sure to get your costume cleaned before Friday, Jo. Your parents would want you to look your best. Appearance is so important. I saw a broadcast from Las Vegas last week, and their costumes were *immaculate*."

"I'll remember," Jo replied, almost laughing aloud. Her costume wouldn't matter a scrap this time! Not when the audience saw TRANSMUTER!

After dinner, before tackling the dishes, she ran upstairs to her room, perched on the edge of her bed, and dialed Kim's number. "Kim—you'll never guess. I've something to show you, the most exciting . . ." Her words tumbled out. "You'll have to come see it. Come as fast as you can."

As usual, Kim sounded breathless and vague. "In the morning?"

"No! Tonight! I *can't wait!*"

"But Jo, I'm going to baby-sit for the Paulsens—you know that little hyena of theirs, Josh. He's a real brat. But they're good pay, and I promised Mrs. Paulson, and she calls me oftener than anyone. If I don't turn up, she might ..."

"Kim! If you *knew!*" Jo thumped a pillow with her free hand.

"Hey, what's up anyway?" Kim sounded annoyed. "You're going off like a fire siren."

"I can't tell you. You'll have to see for yourself. And ... Kim, what time do you have to be there?"

"Eight o'clock." Kim's voice faded. "Look, Jo, we're still eating, and we have pineapple cake. I'll come tomorrow."

"Tomorrow!" Jo gave the telephone an impatient shake. "Listen—it's a long time until eight o'clock. Come for a few minutes."

"Well ... all right. I guess so."

A little later, just as Jo finished loading the dishwasher, she heard Kim's voice in the front hall. "Hey! I'm here. But I have to hurry."

Jo hastily poured detergent into the machine, flipped its door shut, and ran to meet her. "That's all right. We'll hurry." She bounded ahead of Kim up the stairs and into her room, where she closed the door and turned the lever.

Kim's eyes widened. "Wow! Locking the door? *Why,* for silly's sake?"

"You'll see in a minute!" Jo knelt beside the chest and brought out the leather case. "Now . . . *here it is.*" With a flourish she spread the shawl, the gray box, and the directions on the desk.

"It's . . ." said Kim, lifting a corner of the shawl. "It's . . . this scarf is pretty. But the box doesn't look like much. Does it really do something?"

Jo picked up the shawl and shook it out, showing off its vivid red and blue and gold. "Just wait! What shall I put it on?"

"Oh, over there." Kim shrugged and pointed toward the blue leather hassock at the foot of the bed.

"All right. Now—watch!" Refolding the shawl into a small square, Jo laid it on top of the hassock, sat down on the desk chair, and started to press buttons, reading the directions aloud as she went along. "Green. Yellow. It has to be exactly right. Red. Orange. Kim, you're going to be so surprised!"

"Well I hope so. Jo! You're shaking! Are you scared of that little box?"

"Don't mix me up. Yellow. Red. Red." Jo carefully finished the list. *"Abracadabra!"* She pressed the black key—and the hassock was gone.

Kim's mouth fell open. "But . . . but where is it?"

"Right there. Touch it—go ahead. It won't bite."

"Touch it? No, thanks!" Kim shrank into the farthest corner, as close to the wall as she could.

"It'll hold things. Watch!" Jo laid a book on the

hassock, which she could feel but not see, and the book stood there as if suspended in midair.

"What ..." Kim had turned pale. "What happened?"

"This trick is a vanisher! A real one! *Now* do you think the audience will notice it?"

"They'll notice something awful, that's sure. Can you get it back?"

"I think so. I did it before." Jo started through the directions again. "Violet. Indigo. Blue. I do that four times." After working the buttons, which felt familiar now, almost like a calculator, she came to the end. "White." And the hassock reappeared.

"But ... but where *was* it?" Kim demanded. "I didn't see it fly into the closet, or anything."

"I told you, it was there all the time. Didn't you see it holding up the book?"

"Yes, but ... but it's impossible!" Kim was still in the corner, as far as possible from Jo. "I could see the floor right through it! I think I could, anyway."

"You could."

"You mean that little box does something to the shawl that makes it ..."

"I don't know exactly *what* I mean," Jo replied, feeling suddenly cross. Did Kim have to be so suspicious? Couldn't she accept anything without having it all explained, like a stumble-bumble science experiment? "All I know is, this is what happens."

"Every time?"

"I've only tried it twice."

Kim ventured a few steps from the corner, holding her hands behind her. "I don't like that creepy thing. Where did you get it, anyway?"

"From the Cave. Actually, from the back room. It's special." Jo made a circle of her thumb and finger and drew the shawl through it. The material was light and soft, curling into an incredibly narrow twist that slid through her fingers as if it were alive, and while Jo was handling it, she explained what had happened. She described the cold, dusty room, the shelves of tricks, and the old desk; but she didn't mention the secret drawer, or confess that she hadn't told Mr. Paisley the whole story. She didn't even like to think about it. "I was lucky," she finished.

"Lucky? Well ... maybe." Venturing still closer, Kim perched warily on the edge of the bed. "Did it cost much?"

"Five dollars." Jo ran the shawl through her fingers again. "Don't you want to try it? It's fun!"

Kim wrapped her arms tightly across her chest, hanging on to herself. "*Fun!* Ugh! How does it ... ?"

"Kim—honest—I don't know," Jo replied as she folded the shawl into a small square again, with its golden swirls on top, so they would show. "It's crazy. Magic, I guess."

"Magic!" Kim reached out and timidly pressed one of the colored buttons. "There isn't any such thing! Except in books."

"That's what I used to think, too." Jo spoke slowly, groping her way along, trying to understand. "All I know is . . . my math book disappeared, and when it came back it was the same old book as before."

"Weird!" said Kim, with a shudder.

"Yes. But we don't have to understand it, just so we can make it work." Jo paused, imagining herself onstage with a wand and TRANSMUTER, under the bright lights. "We'll have the best act any talent show ever put on."

Kim wrapped her arms around herself again. "*You* will! I don't want anything to do with it."

"We've been a team practically forever!"

Kim silently shook her head.

"*Please!* You're the best assistant anybody could have."

Kim shook her head again.

Jo felt as if a rod of steel had grown inside her, holding her stiff—her back, her neck, all the way to her fingers and toes. "All right. But *I'm* going to do it anyway," she said through rigid lips. "I'd hate myself if I gave up now. If you really won't help me, I'll . . . I'll get one of the other Merlins."

Kim twisted her hands in her lap.

"Or I'll put on the act by myself."

"I'm scared."

"I know. It scares me, too." Jo remembered how she had felt when she first saw that the book was gone. "But I've worked it twice now, and nothing bad happened. And Kim—it'll be a lot more fun with you. Please?"

Kim opened her mouth to reply, swallowed, then moistened her lips with her tongue. "All right, I'll try," she finally whispered. "But I don't like it."

"You won't be sorry!" Jo handed her the directions. "Here—it won't pinch or scratch or make you dizzy or anything. Pretend we're in the show. You read the list and work the buttons while I drape the shawl on something and . . ."

"*Me!* Work those *buttons?* In the *show?*" Kim's voice rose to a frightened squeak.

"Of course! There's nothing to it!" Jo tried to remain patient and helpful. "We'll put it on your assistant's table, behind that little shelf so nobody except you can see it, and you go through the colors. You nod just before black. I'll wave a wand, you press the button, and the objects disappears."

"I don't . . ."

"Try it just once. I'm counting on you."

Heaving a single huge sigh, Kim dragged the chair close to the bed and dropped down on it. "All right. Show me how."

After laying the shawl on her library book, *The Yearling,* Jo put the gray box in Kim's lap and the directions on the bed, near enough for her to read. "Now remember to nod." She picked up a ruler to serve as a wand, and gabbled aimlessly to an imaginary audience while she watched out of the corner of her eyes. Although Kim was still pale, her hands were moving, and in a few moments she nodded.

"Good!" Jo waved the ruler, Kim pressed the black button, and the book disappeared, along with the magazine it was lying on.

"Whoosh!" Kim blew out all her breath. "It didn't feel as creepy as I expected. I guess I can do it after all."

"It was perfect!"

"Was the magazine supposed to go, too?"

"No, but it doesn't matter. I think the shawl was touching them both." Jo tried to remember exactly how it had worked on the hassock and math book. "It acts on everything it touches, whether it hides them or not—I think. Now let's get them back."

It was easier this time. Kim pressed the buttons, nodded, Jo waved the ruler, and the book and magazine reappeared.

"Hey! Just right!" Jo picked up the shawl again. "Next—my lamp."

"Okay." But before Kim could start again, her wristwatch beeped. "Oh! I've got to run."

"Nuts! Just when we're figuring it out. But you come back in the morning, and we'll think up something spectacular. Eight o'clock? Nine?"

"Make it nine. I'll see you then." Gathering up her books, Kim ran down the stairs.

When Kim had left, Jo first thought of calling in Woody and showing him the trick, but decided instead to try it once more by herself. Instead of using the lamp, she selected the stuffed panda, the large one with the scruffy ears, and set it on the chair beside the bed. She shook out the shawl, flung it over the bear, and watched it float down in shimmering folds.

With everything ready, she perched on the bed and began. But after the first few words she decided it would be more professional to memorize the code, so she could work it without reading from the paper. She'd begin at once, with the shorter list.

She read it, repeated it from memory, tucked the directions into her shirt pocket and pressed buttons, saying the colors aloud. "Green. Yellow. Red. Orange. Green. Red. Red."

She waited three seconds.

Black. She pressed it.

Nothing happened. There was the shawl, still in plain sight, and the bulge of the panda underneath.

Well! She thought. Something went wrong! She reread the directions, and immediately noticed that the third color from the last should be yellow, not green, so she slipped the paper into her pocket again, and started again.

"Green. Yellow." Don't hurry! Jo warned herself, moving slowly and thinking her way along. Red. Orange. Now, the one she missed before. Yellow.

She pressed it. Red. Red. Wait three seconds. Black.

She pressed the black button. And she felt a tingly jolt, as if she had knocked the funny bone in her elbow, except that it jarred her from head to toe. The entire room seemed to rise up and settle down, as if it were riding a huge wave, while the posters, the blue curtains, the books and bookcase were spread out in sidewise streaks, like pictures taken from a speeding car.

Jo closed her eyes and braced both hands against the bed, to keep from toppling over. The bed was swirling, too—up and down—and around. But after only a few seconds it all became steady again, and the tingle was gone.

How peculiar! thought Jo. Nothing like this had happened before. She opened her eyes a slit, and then wide. The room was all there, focused again, normal—but the panda had disappeared, along with the shawl and the chair.

Jo jumped up and crowed like Peter Pan. She'd memorized half of the Trick already! Losing the chair was a little more than she'd planned, but she could correct that. As for the tingle and the wave, they hadn't lasted long, and were a small price to pay for a trick as wonderful as this. The important thing was that she could make things disappear without having to depend on the list.

She picked up the little gray box, to bring the panda back.

But she couldn't see it!

Neither could she see her hand, although she could feel it the same as always, right there by her wrist. ... *Her wrist! That was gone, too!*

She moved her arms, wiggled a foot, bobbed her head up and down. They moved, all right, or seemed to, but she couldn't see so much as her little toe. She had disappeared. Vanished, like the math book. TRANSMUTER had gobbled her up!

The Paper with the Squiggly Marks

JO STARED AT THE PLACE WHERE HER KNEES ought to be. They didn't show. Instead of faded jeans, a little lighter at the bend, she could see the rug, with its angular blue lines crisply defined against the white background. Close to the desk was a wadded-up page of math problems, which she tried to poke with her toe. It was hard to steer an invisible foot, but all at once the paper moved, and when she stepped down, it lay flat, as if it had been squashed by a pane of clear glass. Although her foot must be on top of it, the paper showed clearly through her socks—her sneakers—her bones. She could even read what it said.

Jo's heart began to pound. She, Jo, all her long-legged gangling self, had vanished. She could move, she could feel, but instead of her skin and legs and clothes, she saw only empty air. Would she be the same, after she got herself back? *Of course she would! After all, she had the second half of the Trick, and it had worked before.*

But right now she was invisible, and what was that going to do to her? Would it hurt? Had she lost anything? She felt her invisible knee, and it could bend. She gave her invisible arm a pinch, and it stung. She thumped her invisible shoulder, and she could feel the thump. She ran her hand through her hair, counted her fingers, wiggled her toes. Everything seemed to be there.

Moving carefully, she walked across the room and yes, she could balance, turn right, turn left, crouch down and stand again, reach out and touch the desk, although it gave her an odd sensation, like groping for a light switch in the dark. She seemed no heavier and no lighter than usual, and the floor was firm under her feet. Maybe she was coming back already!

But when she looked into the mirror, she saw only the usual furniture, blue curtains, posters, closet door, with some memos Scotch-taped to it. She was sure she was in front of the bed, because she could feel it against the back of her knee. The blue spread, the stuffed animals, the pillows, were all in the looking-glass room, showing through the very place where she stood, as if she weren't there at all. She picked up a ballpoint pen from the desk, and it seemed to soar by itself through the air. She punched the pillow, making a dent in it, and she couldn't see the hand that gave the blow.

Jo dropped to the floor and leaned her invisible self against the wall, with her heart thumping as if she had run a race. She could get herself back— of course she could—just as she had restored the math book and hassock. But she must be slow and careful for once in her life, and think this thing through.

First, how did it happen? Exactly what did she do?

The panda had been on the chair in front of her, the directions in her lap, the gray box in her hands, and the shawl draped over the panda, almost hiding it—she was sure of that. When she closed her eyes, she clearly remembered the way it had floated into place. She'd been beside it, sitting on the bed. So, yes, she must have been so close to the panda's chair that the edge of the shawl was touching her. That was the reason she had disappeared, just as the magazine had disappeared along with her library book, because it was in contact with the shawl.

Therefore, whenever she worked the Trick in the future, she must be extra careful that the shawl touched only the right things. If she did that, if she learned to be careful, she could vanish exactly what she intended to, and nothing more. She could even—Jo gasped—she could even make herself go invisible on the stage, and a magician who did that would become famous! Joanna Rodgers, the Incredible! But be sensible, she warned herself. She mustn't use the Trick until she'd practiced a lot, and had it under control.

And right now she must stop daydreaming, and get herself back. She scrambled to her feet, which felt something like standing up in the dark, fumbled in her pocket, and took out the directions.

She couldn't see them.

She held them against the light, turned them toward the side, moved them closer and farther away. The page was crisp in her hand, and when she wrinkled it, she could hear it crackle, but she couldn't see a single word. Instead, the silver-gray window frame showed through, along with the blue curtains.

All of Jo's plans tumbled into a heap, like a sand castle when a big wave comes. The directions had disappeared, and she'd memorized only half of the trick—the first, the simple half. Could she remember the rest? Violet! Indigo! Blue! They thundered in her ears. Green! Yellow! Orange! They roared, howled at her. That part was easy. And then . . . ?

Everything else was a blank. She flung herself

onto the bed and buried her face in the pillow, crying with great sobs that tore at her throat. How could she have been so careless? She had known that the magazine vanished when the shawl was touching it! Why hadn't she realized how danger-ous a trick like this could be? Why hadn't she no-ticed that the shawl was too close? What was she going to do? The pillow was wet with her tears.

But she gradually became more calm. *Unwind!* she told herself, struggling to sit up. *All you have to do is figure out which buttons to punch.*

When I can't see them? her other self replied.

You know they run along the top of the box, right down the middle. Violet first, then indigo. That isn't hard!

I remember the buttons all right. Violet-indigo-blue-green-yellow-orange-red. Black for vanishing. White for coming back.

Good. Now—concentrate! Figure it out. Then feel your way along.

I'll try.

Tucking the invisible sheet of directions into the shirt pocket she couldn't see, Jo turned the invis-ible box until it seemed to be right-side up, and started the sequence. Violet. She felt for button number one, on the left end. Indigo. Button number two. Blue. Number three. Do it four times. She pressed them carefully, being sure to get it exactly right.

Green. Yellow. Orange. Like the rainbow. She

could remember that, too. But next came a whole lot more, all mixed up. Was it green? Or yellow? She'd done it only twice, and there were so *many!* She hadn't even *counted* them!

She went through a combination that she hoped would work, ending with Blue. Green. Red. Orange. Violet. Indigo. Nothing happened.

She tried again. Blue. Orange. Indigo. Red. Violet. Indigo. Nothing changed.

Jo crouched on the edge of the bed with her face in her hands. Unless she went at this logically and remembered what she'd done, she might run through the same sequences over and over, so she'd better keep track. She had visible paper, but would her writing show? She picked up a pen, and it seemed to hover in the air. She slid a notepad across the desk, and it slithered along as if it could crawl. However, when she scribbled a word, she could see it clearly, so she drew a deep breath and wrote out her first line.

She read it through, pressing buttons. Nothing happened.

She tried another. No better.

By the time she had covered two pages with combinations that didn't work, she threw down the pen and hunched in the chair beside the desk, propping her invisible chin on her invisible fist. *Think!* She told herself. *Figure it out!*

Should she ask Mrs. Forbes for help? Hardly! Forbesy would panic. She'd take Jo to the doctor, or to the hospital, or she'd send for the emergency car. She might even call in the police, which would make a mountain of trouble for Mr. Paisley, because he'd sold her the trick. No, not Mrs. Forbes.

She could call in Woody. *Woody!* Jo grimaced. He'd think it was the biggest game yet, and try to work it on his computer. Besides, Woody knew a lot about mathematics and electronics, but not about magic. He'd be just as stuck as she was.

Her parents? Mom and Dad? It would be a great big relief to talk this over with them, but they didn't know as much about magic as she did, and it would ruin their trip. She could at least act her age, and leave them in peace.

Mr. Paisley? Jo groaned. She'd have to slink into the Cave on her invisible feet.

"Mr. Paisley," she'd have to say. "You can't see me, but I'm Jo—and I'm right here in front of you. Mr. Paisley, I was careless. I did that Trick wrong, and now I've got myself invisible, and the directions, too, and I can't get back!"

She'd have to say more than that! She'd have to tell him about the secret drawer. Even though she hadn't fibbed—quite—she hadn't quite told the truth, either, and Mr. Paisley would know it. He had called her responsible and trustworthy, and had hinted that she could be his assistant this summer; but if he knew she was a sneak, he'd never believe in her again. He'd give the job to somebody else.

And even if she went to him, it wouldn't do any good, because he didn't know anything about TRANSMUTER. "I don't recall a trick of that name," he'd said. "A simple vanisher, of course." Even a magician as wonderful as Mr. Paisley couldn't figure out something he'd never heard of and couldn't see!

So that left Kim, who had done the Trick once, and might remember how. Jo decided to go to the Paulsens', where Kim was baby-sitting, and ask for help.

She slipped the directions out of her pocket and picked up the shawl and control box. Since all of these were invisible, she tucked them inside the leather case, which she could see, and laid it on the bed. She mustn't risk losing them.

Next she put on her denim jacket, but when she glanced into the mirror she saw an apparently empty blue garment, bending and turning, with the leather box danging by itself just below one sleeve. Of course! she thought. The only things that had vanished were those she was wearing or holding when she set off the Trick, and anything else would show. She took off the jacket, and wrapped the control box in the shawl.

Holding them in one hand, Jo opened her door, but stopped. The knob turned, as if by itself! The door swung, on its own! Unless she was super-careful, *somebody* would notice *something,* and she might be caught. What a mess she'd be in then, trying to explain!

She had to see Kim—but by now she was terrified at the thought of leaving the house. Jellyfish! she scolded herself. If you're ever going to fix up this boo-boo, you'll have to develop a backbone. Find out what you can and can't do. Get moving.

All right, she would. And she had learned two Rules for Being Invisible:

One: *Wear only invisible clothes.*

Two: *Carry only invisible objects.*

Leaving her jacket on the bed, she stepped into the hall. She could hear the voices of Mrs. Forbes and Woody, probably in the kitchen, as she inched her way down the stairs, stepping over the creaky third step from the top. At the bottom she drew a deep breath and forced herself to open the outside door.

Although it was early evening, it wasn't yet dark. Before Jo had gone far, she saw Mr. Powers, a neighbor, walking toward her with big steps and swinging his arms, as if he meant to run her down. Where were his manners? she thought at first, then remembered that he couldn't see her. Just in time, she dodged aside and let him pass so close she could hear him breathe. Rule Number Three: *Give people a wide berth.*

When she came to the first intersection she stopped, thinking of herself being hit by a car because drivers couldn't see her; of an accident, with injured people lying in the road; of rescuers hearing her voice but unable to find her to take her to a hospital. If they did find her, the doctors wouldn't be able to see her broken bones, to set them straight. Or X-ray them. Or apply a bandage. She waited a long time before she dared to cross the street.

On the other side, she walked without a sound, clutching the shawl and control box in both hands. She was cold without her jacket. She dodged a boy on a skateboard and was terrified that he might run into her, or hear her and guess that someone was there. She was passed by two joggers in sweat-suits who plunged toward her on thudding feet. By then her heart was pounding and her eyes were so full of tears that she could scarcely see. This was awful! She couldn't possibly go all the way to the Paulsens'! Even if she made it safely, it would scare Kim out of her wits when she answered the doorbell and found a voice without a body. And what about Josh? Would he tell his parents that Kim had been talking to herself, or that a ghost had come onto the porch? Assuring herself that it would be much more sensible to go home and telephone instead, Jo turned around and started back.

She walked most of the way in the grass because it was quieter than cement; and once in the house, she crept up to her room, after making sure that

Woody and Mrs. Forbes were nowhere near the stairs. She dropped into a chair, looked up the Paulsens' telephone number, and dialed it on her extension.

Although Kim answered at once, a child was laughing so loudly in the background that Jo had to shout. "Kim! *Kim!* I'm in an awful mess! You know that ... that thing I have?"

"That thing? Oh ... oh, that! Sure. Do you think I could forget it?" Kim replied, and added to the child, "Josh! Not so *loud*! I can't *hear*! We'll play horsey after a while, but right now keep *quiet*!"

"Can you remember how to do it?" Jo asked.

"Remember? That string of buttons? Well, I guess so. Why? Won't it work?"

"It *works,* all right," Jo grimly replied. "Kim—now listen. This is important. Tell me everything you remember about the order of the colors. The second list, to bring back the ... the ... whatever disappeared."

"Bring it back? Have you lost something?" Kim asked, and then added, "No, Josh! Not on the sofa!"

"Never mind what happened! Just tell me what you know!"

"Well ..." Kim was silent for a moment. "You start with blue, I think. Yes, I'm sure it's blue."

"No!" Jo was still shouting. "I remember how it starts. Violet, indigo, blue—four times. That's easy.

And then green, yellow, orange, like the rainbow. The rest is what I can't do."

"Oh. Well, next comes yellow—no, orange. And then its green. Two greens. And then it's blue again. Or maybe red. There's a red in there somewhere. And I think . . ."

"That can't be right, but I'll try again," said Jo, using the hand she couldn't see to wipe away tears she could only feel. "And Kim, be sure to come over just as fast as you can in the morning. Don't let anything stop you."

"Jo!" Kim's voice quavered. "What's wrong? You sound as if you're in somebody else's space or something." She paused. "Hey, just a minute! Josh is gone!"

After a brief silence her voice came on again. "Into his mom's lipstick, but I've got him settled. Now, what's happening, anyway? What have you . . . ?"

"Never mind." Jo cut her off. "Just come. And Kim—don't wait for me to answer the door. Don't even ring the bell. Keep quiet. Tiptoe in and come straight up to my room, and *please* don't say a single word to anybody about—about anything."

"All right. But Jo, you really do sound funny."

"Funny? That isn't quite the word. *Kim. Don't let me down!*" Jo dropped the telephone into place.

* Kim

JO PACKED THE INVISIBLE PARTS OF THE TRICK
in the leather case, which she could see, tucked it
safely away in the bottom drawer of her chest,
then put on her pajamas. She dropped her T-shirt
and groped for it on the rug, found it easily and
folded it by touch, sleeve to sleeve, leaving it with
the rest of her invisible clothes in a neat pile on
the desk, where she could be sure to find them.
While she was moving around the room, she saw
her reflected pajamas standing up, sitting down,
and bending their arms and legs as if they did it
all on their own. She tried to tell herself it was
funny, but instead of laughing, she flopped down

90

on the bed and curled up in misery.

The Jo she knew was gone. She looked down at herself, where her body must be, and saw only the blue and white pajamas—empty. She was clear as glass, but instead of being brittle like glass, she was warm, and could move and think and feel. Her arms, legs, fingers, toes, and everything on the inside— appendix and tonsils and veins and a thousand other parts she couldn't even name—were more like a lump of soft, clear plastic than a person. She was hardly real.

She heard Woody come upstairs, followed later by Mrs. Forbes. She tried to sleep, but heard the grandfather clock strike eleven—twelve—one— and she was still wide awake. Lists of colors thundered through her head and wouldn't stop. Violet. Indigo. ... Suppose she couldn't undo the Trick— ever! Hearing a plaintive mew, she opened the screen. "Come along, Duchess," she said. "Will you be scared of someone you can only feel?" However, the cat merely lay down in her usual spot, purring.

Eventually Jo drifted into an uneasy sleep, and when she woke up it was a dull morning, with fine mist slanting across the fir branches outside the window. In hopes that the Trick had somehow been undone during the night, she held up her hand, and saw the ceiling through it. She ran to the chest for the leather box, but it was the same as before— heavy, with the design of stars and comets and flowers, and a little scratch across one corner. The control box, shawl, and directions, which she had left in it, were still invisible, so she felt to make sure they were there, then put it all back.

Inching her door open, she crept to the head of the stairs, while the clatter of dishes and smells of breakfast drifted upward. *Bacon!* She drew a deep breath. Scorched, of course. But Woody was having cocoa, which smelled wonderful, and she was *starved*! The minute they had gone, she was going to invade the kitchen and see what she could find.

Back in her room, she started to put on the invisible clothes, but it made her dizzy to see the furniture and floor through them. She couldn't find the sleeves, she pulled on the T-shirt upside down, and finally finished with her eyes closed, which was easier, like dressing in the dark.

While she was doing this, she heard Woody go whistling down the hall, and a few minutes later Mrs. Forbes came puffing up the stairs. Terrified, Jo dived into bed half dressed, pulled a pillow close to her head and the blankets above her ears, and rolled over to face the wall.

The door swung open. "Jo, dear. Are you all right?"

Jo breathed heavily, making the covers go up and down. "Oh, yes—fine," she mumbled, trying to sound sleepy. *Please,* she thought. *Please* see the hump I make in the bed—and don't notice the empty gap where my face ought to be!

As usual, Mrs. Forbes sounded anxious. "Jo dear, I know you had a big day yesterday. But you can have a good rest now, and don't worry about a thing. I'm going to rearrange some shelves at the shop, and Woody is meeting me for church. You can come with him, if you want to."

"Maybe. But probably not." Jo faked a loud yawn and pulled the covers almost over her head.

"That's all right, dear. I know how tired you are. Growing girls need their rest." The door clicked shut, and Jo relaxed.

The house was quiet. The station wagon drove away. Paul Aiken came to work on the computer game. When she thought the coast was clear, Jo crept into the kitchen for a glass of milk, a banana, and some bread and butter, not daring to make toast for fear the boys might smell it.

Safely in her room again, she was about to start eating, but hesitated, and moved to the mirror. Would the food show? Would a white stream of milk trickle by itself down her invisible throat and lie like a puddle in her stomach? Would the banana and toast mix with it in a disgusting glob? As she took the first swallow, she watched her image, and when she could see nothing, she sighed with relief. Food, it seemed, became an instant part of her, vanishing just as she had, and for that one small thing she could be grateful.

Just as she finished the last bite, she heard the front door open and Woody's steps pounding down the stairs.

"I came . . . to see Jo." It was Kim's high voice in the lower hall.

"Well, maybe she'll see you and maybe not. She cut me off flat last night, and she hasn't poked her nose out this morning." Woody sounded cross. "What's wrong, anyway? Yesterday Jo was steaming like a locomotive, and now you are, too."

"We're just a little bit—well, quite a bit—tensed up over the show. And that hill's steep for a bike."

"Hmm. I suppose." Steps sounded again on the stairs.

Almost at once Jo's door swung open. "Quick! Shut the door!" she whispered as Kim came bouncing through, pink-cheeked and breathless.

"Jo . . ." Kim looked around with a puzzled frown. "Where are you?"

"Right here! Beside the desk!" Jo replied with a shaky laugh because Kim looked so funny, standing there with her mouth open. "I'm *invisible.*"

Kim slammed the door and plastered herself flat against it. "You *couldn't* be!"

"No? What do you think I am? A ventriloquist?"

"Well . . ." Kim stared. "Jo, this is really weird! It's . . . I'm scared." Her freckles were standing out on her white face. "If this is a joke, it's a dumb one."

"You're right. It isn't one bit funny." Jo moved

forward and touched her friend's arm, but Kim shrank away. "Look, I'm not going to bite! I'm only me—the same old goony blunderer. And in my usual mess."

"Are you a *ghost*?"

"Umm, not exactly. I just got careless, so ..." While Kim stood by the door, twisting a lock of her red hair, Jo told her what had happened. "And now I don't know how to get myself back."

Kim's eyes were round. "That's *awful*! I never knew an invisible person before. How does it feel? Does it hurt?"

"It feels ... well, it doesn't feel at all. And I can *do* anything. See ..." Jo lifted a book, which apparently rose up by itself and floated down again to land on the desk with a gentle plop. "I'm here, same as always, only you can't see me. I can't even see myself."

"But the book—it showed ..."

"I know. The only invisible things are the ones I was wearing or holding when I set off the trick. It was just my luck that—Kim—the directions were in my pocket."

"So *they're* gone, *too*?" Kim had been pale before, but now she turned whiter still and clapped her wrist to her mouth.

"That's the reason I called you." Did Kim always have to ask so many questions? "You needn't look around like that. You can't see them. And ..." Jo swallowed hard. "Kim, if you ever concentrated in your life, do it now. *Please* remember what they said."

"Let's see. Violet . . ."

"Yes. Then indigo, blue. Four times. And then green, yellow, orange. I know that much."

"Oh-h-h, yes. Now let me think." Kim dropped down on the edge of the bed and crouched there with her face in her hands. When she looked up, she whispered through trembling lips. "Jo, I can't remember another single bit."

"You've *got* to!" Jo felt tears on her cheeks. "I've made page after page of color lists, and tried them, and none of them work. Look . . ." She handed over her papers.

"Maybe . . . white?"

"White's at the end."

"Honest, Jo, I don't know what comes next!" Kim leafed through a few papers, then dropped them onto the bed beside her. "You'll have to get help from somebody else instead of me! Somebody that can do it!"

"Such as . . . ?"

"I don't know. But aren't you scared?"

"Sure. But I'm not going to sit here and cry," Jo stoutly said, as she sat down in the desk chair and folded her arms. That, at least, felt just the same as always, even if she couldn't see any arms to fold!

"We could tell Mrs. Forbes." Kim sounded doubtful.

"*Forbesy!* She'd panic. Send for my folks, and get Mr. Paisley into hot water. No. We won't tell Mrs. Forbes. We'll ..."

An angry red spot flamed in each of Kim's cheeks. "How can you *help* telling her, just answer me that? She knows you live here. What will she say when you come to the table?"

"I won't." Jo started to tap the desk with a pencil. "I wouldn't dare. My fork and spoon would be going up and down. My chair would move in and out all by itself. My glass ..."

"Jo—that pencil! If she sees anything moving around like that, she'll think you're haunted."

"She'll think the whole house is haunted. I could pretend to be a ghost." Jo smiled, but only for an instant. "But that's not the main point right now. The first thing we have to do is figure out how I'm going to exist until I get myself back."

"The garage?" suggested Kim. "You could come into the house in the night, to get food."

"Mmm ... maybe. Or the basement. That would be warmer, and we have an old bed down there."

"But they'd miss you."

"I could say ..." Jo laid down the pencil and rested her chin on her fist. "Kim, I know! Mrs. Forbes is at the shop now, fixing up some shelves, so I'll telephone and tell her I'm going to your house for a few days."

"My folks ..."

"Oh, I won't actually leave. I'll hide out right here. Only Mrs. Forbes won't expect to see me, because she'll think I'm gone."

"Do you think she'll let you?"

"Sure. She'll fuss, but she'll say yes. I'm going to try." Jo picked up her telephone.

Mrs. Forbes listened quietly at first, then made a frightened little clucking sound with her tongue. "I don't know, Jo dear. I want things to be just as if your parents were here. Do they let you stay at Kim's?"

"Oh, yes. Lots of times, and Kim stays with me. Especially during vacation."

"I don't want you doing anything your mother wouldn't approve," Mrs. Forbes replied, and Jo could picture her rubbing her forehead and biting her lips.

"I told you—she always lets me."

"And Kim's mother?"

"She won't mind. She never does," said Jo, trying to sound calm. She turned her back on Kim, who was staring, openmouthed and pale, as the telephone seemed to hang in midair.

"Well . . ." Mrs. Forbes still sounded fluttery and uncertain. "It's hard for me to know. But I guess . . . all right, then. If you're sure."

"We're sure." With a sigh of relief, Jo replaced the telephone. "It's okay," she said. "I'll tell Woody good-bye, just as if I were really taking off."

"Won't he see you?"

Jo felt her lips drawing into a grim smile. "*See me! Fat chance of that!*" She was quiet for a moment. "I know. We'll make a racket as if we're leaving, and then I'll shout that I'm on my way to your house. You'll go, but I'll stay here, and keep quiet. Woody's too busy with his game to pay much attention to us."

A few minutes later they pounded down the stairs, and Jo called from the lower hall. "Bye, Woody. I'm going to Kim's for a couple of days." When he leaned over the upper railing, she started to dodge away, but remembered he couldn't see her. "I told Mrs. Forbes, and she doesn't care."

Woody was staring downward. "Where are you, anyway?"

"Just ... here ... we're leaving now."

"Hmm. Funny. Well ... okay. See you later." He clumped back to his room, and when everything was still again, the girls opened the front door.

The sky was gray, pockets of fog blanketed the surrounding mountains, and the ocean, far below, was a silvery sheet broken with white flecks. The wind was cold, swishing through the pine trees, whipping their branches and spitting a fine mist. Jo, however, hardly noticed. She stood forlornly on the front steps and watched Kim ride her bicycle down Madrona Lane, around the corner, and out of sight. Kim was the only person on earth who knew what had happened, and now she was gone.

 # Woody

BACK IN HER OWN ROOM, JO DROPPED DOWN on the edge of the bed and clamped her hands between her knees. If she returned to the Cave and searched it well, perhaps she could find another TRANSMUTER and read its directions. Could she—invisible—make it all the way to Old Town? Did she dare? It was so far, and her heart hammered at the thought of meeting so many people, of going in and out of stores, braving the traffic. Before tackling it, she'd try another short walk close to home, and see if she could manage better this time. The Cave wasn't open on Sunday morning, but Wright's grocery was, and that would be a good place to start.

100

On a day like this Jo needed something warm, so she decided to see whether she could turn her jacket invisible. Green—yellow—red—yes, she remembered the first, the shorter list. She took the leather case out of the drawer, put her jeans jacket on the bed, and laid the shawl, which she couldn't see, on top. After feeling around its edge to be sure it wasn't touching the bedspread, she sat down with the control box, chilly and hard in her hand.

Green. Fourth from the end. Closing her eyes so she wouldn't have to look at emptiness, she fumbled for the key and pressed it.

Yellow. Next to green. Count carefully. She went through the list, touched black—and the jacket disappeared. She could work that much, at least. Finding it awkward to put on a garment she couldn't see, she closed her eyes, groped for the collar, and shoved her arms into the sleeves. She was ready to start.

Outside again, Jo stood on the front steps and looked at the street in front of her, huge and menacing, dull in the gray mist. She *couldn't* go out there, not while she was like this. Someone might run into her! Or walk up behind her! Or hear her footsteps! Madrona, her own town, where she had lived all her life, had become a terrifying place, booby-trapped with hazards and overrun with people who might hear her or see her move something. If she made a mistake—just one—the tiniest one—

it would land her in a barrel of trouble, or she might cause an accident that would hurt other people.

But the only sensible plan she could think of was to return to the Cave and look for a copy of the directions, and that meant she must learn to go places by herself. *I can do it!* she mumbled. *I will.* Clenching her hands, she took a timid step into the cold mist.

This time she met no joggers and no one on skateboards, but as she approached the black dog, Domino, who lived in the next block, he trotted toward her and sniffed at her heels. She and Domino had been friends for a long time; so she looked around to be sure they were alone, then whispered, "It's all right, Dommie."

He laid back his ears and sniffed again, while she tried to scratch his head in the way he always liked. He didn't like it now, but whimpered at the first touch, ran around her in a circle, raised his muzzle toward the sky, and started to howl.

Almost at once the man who owned him appeared on the porch. "Hey, Dommie—what's wrong?"

Domino howled again, and Jo began to run, keeping to the lawn, where her footsteps were silent.

"Come on, boy. Come on in. We can't have a rumpus like that, disturbing the neighbors! What's got into you, anyway?" The owner clapped his hands. "Here!"

After one more long-drawn howl, Domino scuttled into the house, and Jo slowed to a walk. Rule Number Four: *Keep away from dogs.*

In the next block, she was about to enter Wright's grocery but remembered just in time that if she opened the door it would appear to be moving itself. So she waited for the next customer, followed along, and even though she had to hold the door open for an extra moment, nobody seemed to notice.

She stood beside the cash register while Mr. Wright figured purchases, counted out change, and chatted with his customers about the weather, baseball, and the fishing fleet. Being careful not to touch or move anything, Jo listened without much interest until he mentioned the campaign for a community swimming pool.

"Swimming! Who needs it?" the customer exclaimed. "Folks don't want to throw away all that money!"

Jo stiffened. Didn't the silly woman understand that everybody needed exercise, and the town swimming pool was too small? But she, Jo, couldn't say a word! Rule Number Five, and she detested it: *Don't speak out, no matter what!* Even though it was fun to listen to a conversation, it was positively gruesome not to be able to reply! She was glad when another customer came, so she could slip through the open door.

While she was in the store the mist had turned to a heavy rain, hiding the mountains and bay and falling cold on Jo's face. As she trotted along, she happened to glance toward her legs. It was as if two empty columns were swinging back and forth, back and forth, making air pockets that the rain couldn't enter. She looked at her body—another empty space—and when she held out her hand, water stood up on it like drops on a window pane. Jo was afraid that someone might notice this clear, glassy, vacant hole, surging through the rain, so she broke into a run.

By the time she reached home, she was shivering, but she leaned in relief against the inside of the door. She had done it—had taken a real walk, without causing any trouble. She listened for sounds and decided that Woody and Mrs. Forbes hadn't returned yet, so she hastily pulled off her damp jacket and laid it on a chair in the living room, then went to the kitchen to mix a mug of cocoa. She heated it in the microwave, which left no evidence, took it upstairs, and started to write out lists of colors, recording them as she had before, and trying them out.

Violet. Indigo. Blue. ... She was still at it when she heard Mrs. Forbes and Woody come in. All at once she remembered that her jacket was still downstairs, on the chair where Mrs. Forbes sat every evening while she watched her favorite programs on the full-sized set. If Forbesy found it! If she sat on a damp something she couldn't see . . . !

Jo opened the door and listened as footsteps went back and forth, up and down the stairs, into Woody's room and out again. After what seemed like an eternity, everything was quiet except a sub-dued murmur of voices and rattle of dishes. This meant that Woody and Mrs. Forbes were at the table, Jo decided to go after her jacket. She in-tended to pick it up fast and scurry back to her room, but she stopped in the lower hall when she heard her own name.

"Jo's taking this talent show much too seriously," Mrs. Forbes said. "I'm afraid she's overworking."

"She likes it. She'll be all right." Woody didn't seem concerned. "She's really got a pretty good brain."

A "pretty good brain"! Jo bristled. She'd take that up with him as soon as she got herself straightened out. She stepped to the doorway, where she could glare at him, and just then—perhaps because she was hungry—her stomach growled. "Oh!" Catching her breath, she darted away so quickly that she bumped into a chair.

"Woody—I heard something!" Mrs. Forbes exclaimed.

"Just a creak. Houses do it sometimes."

"You're probably right. But I'll have a look." While Jo stood motionless against the wall, Mrs.

Forbes pattered past, close enough for her best, dark-blue Sunday dress to brush against Jo's invisible leg. "Hello! Anybody there?" She peered into the living room, listened at the foot of the stairs, then returned to the table. "I guess you're right, Woody. It was just the house." She began to talk again, while Jo cautiously retrieved the jacket and stole back to her room.

There she sat down at her desk with the shawl and gray box and started to work out another list. *Violet. Indigo....* Concentrating on the invisible buttons, she didn't see the door open; but when she heard a cough and looked around, Woody was there, tall and thin in the doorway, grinning and eating an apple. "Jo! Hey, Jo! What's up?"

Jo held her pen still. If she moved it, even half an inch, he'd be sure to notice.

"I'm not blind, you know, or deaf," Woody continued. "I can see your glass on the desk, and it wasn't there when I left the house. Your bed's wrinkled, too, and it was straight this morning while you were on the porch, leaving for Kim's. I came in and looked. And I heard you. ..."

Jo forgot to be still. "You *heard* me!" she exclaimed, then clapped her hand over her mouth. She'd really torn it now!

"Your *stomach*," Woody explained in a dignified tone, as he closed the door. "Nobody else's sounds quite like yours. Musical, almost. Also, you knocked against that chair in the hall. I didn't let on to Forbesy, but I guessed." Striding to the closet, he brushed his hand across the clothes that were hanging there. "You might as well come out. I'll find you."

At that, Jo dropped the pen. It would be *so good*—such a heavenly relief—to tell Woody the whole story. "I'm here, all right," she said. "Only don't give me away. Promise?"

"Hey!" He stared in her direction. "How in heck do you do that? Are your throwing your voice?"

"Not exactly. I just ..." Jo jumped up, tipping over the chair with a thump. "Woody—it's awful! *I've got myself invisible!*"

"Invisible!" Woody dropped his apple and didn't seem to notice it rolling across the floor. "Come off it! I'm not quite a fool!" He stalked over to the chest, peered into the corner behind it, knelt and looked under the bed.

As soon as he stood up, Jo started to explain, but Woody interrupted. "You're nuts!" He folded his arms and glared in the direction of her voice.

"It's true!" She touched his shoulder with her invisible hand. "Feel that?"

He whirled and tried to grab her, but only brushed her wrist. "Something's there, all right!" he admitted.

"It's me."

Speechless, Woody dropped onto the hassock,

rumpling his hair and shaking his head, while Jo told him everything except the way she had deceived Mr. Paisley. "And I can't get myself back!" She longed to burst into sobs and howl and kick her feet. "I've tried ... such a lot ... of lists."

"Lists?"

"These." Jo handed him the papers, and told him what they were.

He scanned them, then sat with his arms crossed and a dazed look in his eyes. "Hmm. Weird. So now ..."

"I've got to get back."

"Well ... sure." He sounded doubtful. "There must be a way."

"There's a way, all right—on the direction sheet. But that's invisible, too. Woody—is there anything you can do?"

"Mmm—I can bring you something to eat. Keep Forbesy off. And the main thing ..." Frowning, he looked at her papers again. "I can try to figure out those invisible directions. Okay?"

Jo sagged against the back of her chair. She had been determined to work it out by herself, without telling anybody, but she was scared—and maybe he could help her. "All right, Woody," she said, almost in a whisper. "What do we do first?"

The Only Way

WOODY STOOD IN THE MIDDLE OF THE FLOOR, reading Jo's pages of lists. "Hmm. You've got the right idea—sort of—but not much of a system. Let's see, now. Tell me as much as you can, and I'll write it down. You said your control box has colored buttons? What are they?" His hair was hanging over his forehead, and he brushed it back.

"The ones in the rainbow," Jo replied, trying to sound sensible. "And black. And white on the underside."

"Hmm. Those lists that you follow when you work it—do you remember any at all? Even parts of them?"

"I know some—how to make them disappear. But to bring them back ..." Jo buried her face in her hands. "I can't remember."

"How long are they? Six words? Ten? Twenty?"

"A whole lot. Maybe—maybe ten. Or twenty." Why hadn't she copied the directions in her notebook? In a dozen notebooks? *Why hadn't she learned the long list first?*

"You didn't count them? Seems as if you'd know that much."

"I'm sure *you* would." Jo's voice was rising. "But I'm not a genius, you know. Just an ordinary ..."

"Hey, cool it! We've got enough troubles without you getting sore. I just thought ... oh, well." He was silent, while Jo sat at her desk and stared at the window, where wet fir branches were tossing in sudden gusts of wind.

In a moment Woody took a step toward the sound of Jo's voice. "Are you still here? This is nutty, talking to space." He looked at the bed, the chair, the floor. "Anyhow, tell me whatever you can—and I'd better keep track. Your pen?" She handed him a ballpoint and notepad. "Boy! It sure is spooky, seeing them come at me through the air. When we get this trick ironed out, I'd like to try it myself. I could give the guys a real shock."

"Woody! It isn't *funny*!" Didn't he care about anything except his scientific ideas? Couldn't he realize how she felt, trapped by this awful thing? "I'm *in-*

visible! I can't talk to anybody except you and Kim. I have to go sneaking around. Maybe I can't ever get myself back! Maybe . . ." Jo felt as if she would strangle on her own words. "Maybe I'll be a freak all my life! I'm scared!"

Woody's voice turned gentle. "I know. It must feel rotten. But we'll get it." He dropped onto the floor, flipped the notepad to a fresh sheet, and while Jo recited the colors of the rainbow, he jotted them down. "Good. That gives us a framework," he said then. "And now, tell me everything you remember about the directions. Everything, however small."

Trying to be as matter-of-fact as he was, Jo began. "There are two lists. I memorized the first one—green, yellow, red, orange, yellow, red, red. After that . . ."

"Hey! Not so fast."

Jo repeated it more slowly, and then continued, "I know part of the rest. It starts violet, indigo, blue—four times. Then green, yellow, orange. That much is easy—like the rainbow." She put her hands over her eyes, trying to concentrate. "But Woody, I've thought and thought, and I can't remember another bit, except the last two. They're violet, indigo."

"Mmm . . ." He scribbled silently, and then continued, "I could work out every possible combination with my computer, and one of them would have to be right; but there would be an awful lot. There are seven colors. To add one button to the part you know would take seven tries. To add another, you'd have to put the colors, one at a time, after each of those seven. Seven times seven tries— forty-nine. Follow me?"

"Sort of."

"Don't sweat it. But if you want to add still another color, multiply all those forty-nine by seven; and then, every time you add another button, you multiply by seven again."

"That must be—quite a few," Jo faltered, feeling bewildered.

"Quite a few! It's a heck of a lot! Have you got a calculator?"

"Sure." She rummaged for the one she kept in her desk drawer, handed it over, and huddled in her chair while he manipulated the controls and jotted down answers. "There. Have a look. And this is only eight buttons. You might need more." He ripped off the page and handed it to her.

To add 1st button:	$7 \times 1 = 7$
2nd	$7 \times 7 = 49$
3rd	$49 \times 7 = 343$
4th	$343 \times 7 = 2,401$
5th	$2,401 \times 7 = 16,807$
6th	$16,807 \times 7 = 117,649$
7th	$117,649 \times 7 = 823,543$
8th	$823,543 \times 7 = 5,764,801$

"Over five million! No wonder my silly little lists didn't work!" It was awful, Jo thought. Five million tries! "What'll we *do*?"

Woody scowled at the list. "It's going to be really tough to find the combination this way. Worse than I expected. Actually, Jo, your best bet is to go back to Paisley, and get him to help you."

"He can't. And besides . . ." Jo looked desperately at the window, where rain was drumming on the glass. "I was . . ." She swallowed hard, then forged ahead. "I was sneaky. I was afraid he wouldn't sell it to me."

"So?"

"The Trick was in an old desk. In a secret drawer. And I . . . I didn't tell him that."

"Fibbed a little?"

"*No!* I didn't say a single word that wasn't true. I just didn't explain it all."

"No difference."

"I know." Jo could feel her shoulders sag. "I'm in a mess, and it serves me right. Woody, he sort of hinted that I might be his assistant this summer, but if he knows what I did . . ."

"Yeah." Woody nodded. "I get it."

"Anyway, telling him wouldn't do any good. The Trick was with the stuff from that Capricorn shop, and he didn't even know he had it. He called it a simple vanisher."

"How about that other fellow—the guy that sells kites?"

"Sidney?" Jo shook her head and suddenly remembered that Woody couldn't see it. "He doesn't know any magic at all."

"Okay, okay. I guess we're on our own. Let's get with it." Woody ran his hand through his hair, causing it to stand out in all directions. "Let's see now. If this is just a string of miscellaneous colors, we're sunk. But if it's a code based on a word, as lots of them are, then each color stands for a letter of the code word." He scratched his head again. "If that's the way it works, those first three colors might represent a short word used four times, and the rest of the colors might be a longer word. So— did you say the box says 'Transmuter' on the cover?"

"Yes. In fancy letters."

"Good. A word repeated four times, and then 'Transmuter.' Let's fit it to the colors you remember. Like this." Frowning, he scribbled again, and when he was through he handed Jo the page. He had written:

—— —— ——

VIOLET   INDIGO   BLUE   *(four times)*

T	R	A	N	S	M	U	T	E	R
GREEN	YELLOW	ORANGE	—	—	—	—	—	VIOLET	INDIGO

"Get it?"

"Sure. But there's a lot left out!"

"Yeah. The whole middle section. It doesn't work, anyway, because we've got two *r*'s—see?" He pointed to them. "One says yellow, but the other says indigo, and they have to be the same."

"Oh-h-h!" Jo let her breath out in a sigh that felt like a collapsing balloon. "I was *sure* that was the right one."

"Lighten up, now. There are plenty of other words. If it ends with 'er,' it might be 'disappearer.' Or 'vanisher.' And if you're right about that last violet, indigo, then the short word must start the same, which would make it 'er,' too." He chewed on the end of his pencil, then doubtfully added, "It could be 'era,' if it's a time machine."

"Time machine! Woody, this isn't a machine! Especially a *time* machine! I'm here! Right now!" Jo picked up a book and waved it wildly, so its cover flapped like wings. She picked up her chair and made it soar across the room, then set it down with a thump. "The person doing that is me! Anything that can do this to me is magic! *Real magic!*"

Woody folded his arms and leaned against the base of the desk, long legs stretched out across the blue carpet. "You don't actually buy that guff, do you?" He stared toward the bed, where Jo was sitting. "Your voice comes from there, so that's where you must be. You're real, even if we can't see you. This trick is real, too, but it sure isn't magic."

"It is! It would be *totally impossible* for it to be

anything else," Jo stubbornly insisted.

"Impossible!" Woody almost shouted it. "Nothing's impossible. When people say something's impossible, that means it hasn't been discovered yet. That guy in the Capricorn shop probably swiped this from a scientific lab somewhere. They're all over the world, diving into stuff you and I wouldn't think of in a thousand years. Plenty of things seem like magic, unless you know what they are."

"Such as ... ?"

"Radio, snatching sounds out of air that looks empty! TV, getting sound and pictures both! Do you call them magic?"

"Of course not. But *vanishing* is *different.* Nothing as impossible as this could be a plain machine." Jo thumped the bed with her fist, making dents that seemed to appear without any cause.

"You think so?" Woody began to doodle geometric shapes, all interlaced. "How about satellite communication? Sound goes out hundreds of miles and bounces back. Computer chips? The new ones make millions of connections in one second. *Millions!* Do you know how much a million is?"

"I heard you." Jo felt almost angry. "It's a lot."

Woody was staring off somewhere, with his eyes glistening, and a smile at the corners of his mouth. "I'll say it's a lot," he said. "Lab workers are doing other things, too. They've found material that conducts electricity without losing any. *Any!* People used to think that was impossible, and now they're talking about trains that run on it without touching the ground. Scientists used to say there were four forces—and now some of them think they've found a fifth, maybe more. It repels objects instead of attracting them."

"Woody . . ." Jo said, but he plowed ahead without listening.

"Plenty of things haven't been figured out yet, but they will be. To say we can't understand something *yet,* that's good sense. But to say it's impossible—nope! Nobody knows. And that's the way with your trick. Vanishing may turn out to be pretty basic, when we learn how. Maybe it's just a system for sending light rays through things instead of letting them bounce back."

He started to scribble again. "Transmuter. That's a bummer—cross it off. There are plenty of words like it that we haven't tried."

"Name some," muttered Jo.

"Transmutes. Transmuting. Vanish. Disappear. Activate. If we run out, we'll use a dictionary." Woody scrambled to his feet. "Where do you keep the Trick? Is all of it together?"

"Yes. In the back of the bottom drawer, under my pj's. Always in the same place, so I won't lose it." Jo brought him the leather box, handed him the invisible parts, and explained what they were.

"Good." He ran his finger over the invisible buttons of the control box and gave it all back. "I won't forget. And now I'm going to think up all the promising words I can, and in the morning I'll try them on the box and shawl. While I'm doing that, you go to the Cave and hunt around, just in case there's another trick like this one, with directions you can read."

"I *couldn't*! It's away down in Old Town!" Jo thumped her fist into the nearest pillow. "Woody, I've been out twice, not very far, and it was *awful*! Skateboarders almost ran into me. Drivers can't see me. I can't let myself make a sound. Even Dommie—good old Dommie—howled at me. I *can't* go so far!"

"You'd rather stay like this?"

Jo felt tears running down her invisible face. "*No! Of course* not! But, Woody—it's dangerous! And suppose Mr. Paisley catches me?"

"When he can't see you? He won't know you're there."

"No? With things moving around on the shelves? And the drawers sliding open and shut?"

"Look." Woody groped in her general direction, then drew his hand back. "Jo—wherever you are—try to think straight. The Cave is your best bet."

Woody was right, of course, thought Jo. Even though it wasn't very likely that another TRANSMUTER was there, she might find something that would help him figure out the code. And still she was terrified. "Woody," she murmured. "Could we do it together? You keep Mr. Paisley busy, so he won't notice me, while I . . ."

"Nope."

"Please?"

He stopped scribbling and looked toward her voice, his dark eyes serious behind his glasses. "Listen, Jo—I'm going to spend my time cracking that code. Ask Kim to go with you. She could keep Paisley busy while you scratch around."

"Kim? She'd be scared to pieces."

"She's the only one besides you and me that knows what's going on. Give her a call."

"I told you . . ." Jo folded her arms across her chest and looked through herself at the blue bedspread. How could she face it, going to the Cave, with Mr. Paisley watching and listening? With so many people close by? Traffic bearing down on her, not knowing she was there? And still . . .

"All right, Woody—if it's the only way." She picked up the telephone. "I'll try."

*⋆ The Back Room Again

THAT EVENING AFTER MRS. FORBES WAS SAFELY absorbed in a game show, Jo made a cheese sandwich, which she put into a Ziploc bag. Upstairs again, she laid the sandwich and a set of clean clothes on the bed, covered them with the shawl, and ran them through the first part of the trick, turning them invisible.

With this done, she took a shower. She couldn't see herself—just the tiles and chrome fixtures, showing through as if she were made of glass. But real glass would have a shine, a form, an outline, while nothing of her showed except the water bouncing off, as if a Jo-shaped plastic balloon were standing in the spray. She tried not to think about it as she put on her pajamas; but after she crawled into bed, she couldn't forget the weird effect, and she was still wide awake when Duchess howled to be let in.

Early the next morning, before anyone else was stirring, Jo dressed in her clean but invisible clothes, crammed the sandwich into the jacket pocket, and slipped out of the back door. Although the storm was over, the ivy was shining wet, and round drops of water quivered at the tips of the pointed rhododendron leaves. She took a long look at the fog-draped mountains, then slipped into the garage and climbed into the back seat of the station wagon.

A few minutes later, the electric door opener rumbled and Mrs. Forbes took her place in the driver's seat. She turned on the radio news and drove at a slow, majestic pace, while Jo sat stone-quiet, making sure she didn't scrape a foot, or cough, or even breathe hard.

Just before they reached the long downhill slope, Mrs. Forbes stopped to pick up a neighbor who was waiting at a bus stop with her six-year-old son, Tommy, on their way to visit a friend. The neighbor climbed in beside Mrs. Forbes and installed the boy in the rear seat, with Jo.

Jo had occasionally been Tommy's baby-sitter, and she watched warily while he brought a Ping-

Pong ball out of his pocket and began to toss it from hand to hand. He played quietly until he missed a catch, and the ball bounced back at him, off Jo's knee.

"Hey! Weird!" he exclaimed. After retrieving his ball, he tossed it again toward Jo's side of the car, but she dodged, so it missed her and struck the door with a gentle thwack.

His mother turned around. "Tommy! You mustn't play ball in the car. You know that."

"It bounced funny," the child replied.

"We were going around a corner, and we hit a little bump," his mother explained. "It's all right."

"But it *did*! I *saw* it! I heard it, too!"

"Of course you did! I told you, we turned the corner. Now you be a good boy. We mustn't bother Mrs. Forbes."

As soon as his mother had turned away, Tommy began to play with the ball again. He threw it toward Jo, reached for it, and she barely managed to dodge. The next toss grazed her elbow. *Please*, Mrs. Forbes. *Please hurry!* she silently pleaded. She was sure she would be caught, but a powerful truck came roaring up the hill, and just as they met it, under cover of the noise, she scrambled over the back of the seat into the cargo space and crouched beside the tailgate.

As usual, Mrs. Forbes parked behind the Jolly Rodgers, and Jo scrambled out of the car and hurried along Old Main Street, stepping off the sidewalk whenever she met anyone. In the last block she found Kim gazing into the window of the Surf Riders' Swim Shop, next door to the Cave. "Kim— I'm here," she whispered.

Kim jumped, then replied without turning around, "Jo, what am I supposed to do? I've never heard of such a mess."

"Don't worry. Just help me get through the door to the back room and keep Mr. Paisley busy while I look for a trick."

"Swipe a trick! You can't do that!" Kim stiffened, twisting a lock of her red hair around her finger.

"Not *swipe* it!" Jo tried to sound more reasonable than she felt. "I don't want to *take* anything. I'll just hunt around for something like Transmuter, and read the directions."

"I thought you'd already checked out everything there."

"Yes, but I wasn't looking for it then. I might have missed it." Jo touched Kim's arm, and Kim shrank away. "Hey! I'm not going to hurt you! And Kim . . ."

"Why don't you tell Mr. Paisley about it? He'd help you."

"Tell Mr. Paisley! That would ruin everything! If he finds out what a fool I've been . . ." What a sneak, Jo thought, but she didn't say it. "Besides, he doesn't know anything about Transmuter. He told me so himself. Please, Kim. It's my only chance."

Kim replied almost in a whisper, "All right. I'll try."

They entered the shop, where Mr. Paisley was sitting in the far corner, leaning back in his chair with his feet resting on the shiny nickel rim of the stove and his glasses perched on the end of his nose. He was reading *Conjurer's Digest,* but when Kim stopped just inside the door, he stood up and shuffled toward her, smiling and rubbing his hands together.

"Kimberly! One of my expert young magicians!"

Kim clasped her hands behind her back, so tightly her knuckles turned white. "I'm looking for . . . for something really special," she quavered. "We have to do an act in the big talent show, Jo and I . . ."

"I know about that. I was at the tryout, and mighty proud." Mr. Paisley shoved his glasses into place. "An outstanding job. I've already advised Joanna to be wary about making changes. You have a good act, so stick to it." His eyes were beginning twinkle, and he reached toward Kim's jacket collar. "What a lovely scarf!" With a flourish he brought his hand away, and it was holding a filmy blue silk, patterned with yellow sunbursts that blended into green.

Kim touched her collar and giggled, while Jo, who had already begun her search, was so interested in watching Mr. Paisley that she jarred a box.

Mr. Paisley turned his head toward the sound.

"Oh—that's neat, Mr. Paisley!" Kim exclaimed in a high, frightened voice. "I wish I could do it, too." She stepped between him and the shelf where Jo was working. "Mr. Paisley, Jo and I are supposed to have a ... a longer act ... for the next show. So she asked me to look for the very best trick you have."

Somber again, Mr. Paisley folded the silk into a small square. "The very best? No, I don't think so, Kimberly. Some of them are much too hard for such young magicians, however talented. And ..." He looked around. "Isn't Joanna with you? Surely she wants a part in the planning."

"Oh, she ..." Kim hesistated, then plunged gamely ahead. "She couldn't come today, so I said I'd try. She's ... we're ... I'll tell her what we find."

Mr. Paisley tucked the silk into his pocket. "Still seeking the easy road? Well, it would be wiser for her to make the search herself, but we'll do our best. Maybe over here ..." He started toward the shelf where Jo was working.

Kim grabbed his elbow. "Let's try those bigger ones." She edged toward the opposite side of the shop. "And please—will you help me, Mr. Paisley? I'm not very good at picking them out."

He stared at Kim with a puzzled smile, glanced toward Jo's shelf, and then turned back. "I understand—a show of that magnitude frightens you. So, have you seen the Butterfly Caper? It's effective, but not very difficult." He walked toward the other wall.

For the next half hour, while Kim kept Mr. Paisley busy, Jo continued her surreptitious search. The Cave was warm, and she felt choked in its dusty air. The postman brought a handful of mail. A customer came in; a second, a third. A fishing boat passed with a hollow blast of its horn, and one of the fishermen shouted to someone on shore.

Jo worked her way along the shelves of boxes, reading their names and raising the covers of some so she could peer inside. After she finished, she crept to the door of the back room and tried its handle; but as she expected, it was locked.

The next time Mr. Paisley was busy with a customer, she edged close to Kim and whispered, "I'm through."

Kim only nodded, but in a moment she stepped toward the door and called out, "I'm going now, and thank you, Mr. Paisley, for all that help. I'll tell Jo about the Butterflies, and the Magnetic ... the Magnetic ... ?"

"Gloves. And be sure to ask her to come in herself. Maybe I can give her a new pointer or two." He turned back to his customer, while Kim left, holding the front door open long enough for Jo to slip through.

This end of Old Main Street was nearly deserted, and the girls hurried toward the park. "You were just great, Kim," Jo said, keeping her voice low.

"Did you find anything?" Kim whispered back.

"No luck." Jo kept to the outside edge of the walk, where Kim wouldn't bump her. "Nothing a bit like Transmuter—but I expected that. So I'm going back this afternoon, and *somehow* I'm going to get into the storage room."

"But ... Mrs. Paulsen ..."

"I know. You have to baby-sit Josh, but that's all right. You've helped with the hard part, and I can manage the rest on my own."

At the end of the street they entered the city park, which was warm today, with patches of sunlight dappling the ground. They dropped down beside a large clump of rhododendrons near the water, which was at low tide, exposing a narrow strip of sand on the opposite side of the Neck. A stick-legged heron was standing among the reeds, and they watched it lunge into the air and fly majestically toward the bay, long legs trailing.

The girls hurried through their lunch. Presently Kim left for her baby-sitting job, while Jo stuffed her empty sandwich bag, still invisible, into her pocket, and returned to the Cave. There she waited on its step, and when the next customer came, she managed to slip through before the door swung shut.

She stood in the back corner while Mr. Paisley sold a set of Linking Rings to the customer, and a deck of cards to another. After the last sale, he took his long coat and blue knit scarf off a peg on the rear wall and put them on, buttoning the coat with care and winding the scarf twice around his throat. "On my way now. Have to see my dentist," he called from the hallway.

"Right! I'll keep your castle," Sidney called back, and Mr. Paisley was gone.

Alone in the Cave, Jo heard the bell over the door jingle, and someone go into the kite shop. Later, three Merlins appeared, and Sidney ambled down the hall to wait on them. When the Merlins left, he did too, and everything was quiet except a long, mournful tune whistled by Sidney, out of sight.

For some time nothing happened. Nobody came shopping. Nobody entered the back room. Jo had decided it was a wild-goose chase and was standing by the window, ready to leave, when a sleek gray car drove up and a square-shouldered stranger got out. Jo heard the bell and a voice that said, clipping off the words, "Sid Larrance? You here?"

"At your service." A moment later Sidney came into the Cave, followed by the man, who was wearing such a neat gray suit and strode forward so firmly that Jo was sure he must be important. A magician, perhaps, come for a special trick?

"McElroy's my name," he said. "Gave you a call last week. Remember?"

Sidney grinned and arched his bushy eyebrows. "Natch! I never forget a face—or a voice. Still interested?"

The man stopped with his feet planted wide apart. "Hmm. Maybe. I'll have a look, anyhow."

"Good! Excellent! As I said, this has to be under the table. And the price is high."

"All right, all right—cash on the barrelhead. But I've got to be shown."

"No problem." Sidney took a ring of keys from his pocket and opened the narrow door. The back room! thought Jo. This was her chance! She followed so closely she almost stepped on the stranger's heel, but he didn't seem to notice, and she tiptoed without a sound down the three worn steps.

The room was as dim and lofty as she remembered, its floor quivering with the slap of the waves underneath. Although Sidney started forward, the man waited, rocking slightly from his heels to his toes. "Not too fast," he said. "How does this gadget work, anyhow? You never did explain."

Sidney jingled the keys against his palm. "The only guy that knew that was Henry Blake—and he's dead. I never tried it out, but Henry told me all about it."

Henry Blake! *Blake!* thought Jo. Henry Blake was the man from Capricorn! Did Sidney know him?

The stranger folded his arms. "Hmm. It still doesn't sound reasonable. But you say it does the job?"

"Right. Henry was a squirrel, but he was smart, and he wouldn't lie. He said you just follow the directions. Can't miss."

"I'll believe it when I see it. But all right. Where is it?"

"This way." Sidney led the man past all the shelves, stopped beside the rolltop desk, and bent toward the lower left-hand drawer.

At this Jo stood as silent as stone, not daring to move. Had Sidney already found TRANSMUTER? If so, why had he brought a stranger back here? To make a deal? Was he planning to sell TRANSMUTER without telling Mr. Paisley? That was sneaky! And what did they want it for? Nothing good, she was sure of that. Sidney was fun, but she remembered that sometimes he cheated his customers, and all of a sudden she was frightened. Holding her breath, she fled to the rear of the room.

Grinning until his mustache bristled, Sidney knelt to pull out the drawer on the left, and then the secret one behind it, lifting it high. However, his grin faded at once, and his eyes opened wide. "Hey!" he exclaimed. "It's empty."

"Yeah. I thought so," the man growled, standing at his elbow. "A fishy idea, right from the word go."

"It's got to be here!" Sidney insisted. "Nobody knew about it except me. Not even Paisley—

especially not Paisley." He turned the box upside down and shook it, then pulled out all the others. "This room's always locked up tight. He and I have the only keys."

The stranger snorted. "Maybe. But somebody got in—if you're leveling with me."

"I am." Sidney's voice turned harsh. "And I know who's got it—that girl." He lifted his upper lip in a snarl. "Paisley let her in here. I saw her, and found the door open."

He's furious! With me! thought Jo. He's my friend—at least he was. We always joked together. But now . . .

Sidney stood up and slapped the dust from his hands, with his eyebrows drawn into such a scowl that Jo's heart began to pound. She must run—run—get away before he heard her breathe. Or she stumbled. Or bumped something.

While she huddled in her corner, Sidney shoved the desk drawers back into place and thrust his long fingers into the cubbyholes, one by one. He pulled out something and looked at it closely, then flung it down and started to stride around the room, peering into shelves, moving boxes, jerking out sofa cushions and running his hand into the dusty crevices. The stranger stumped along behind him, feet clattering on the wooden floor.

"Keep it quiet!" Sidney barked. "No use advertising where we are."

All at once he rushed toward the rear of the

room, close to the corner where Jo stood with her feet braced, ready to run. But he merely shook a portion of the wall, and Jo noticed that it was a sliding door as high as the ceiling, fastened by massive iron hooks. Grasping one of these, Sidney gave the door a mighty jerk, but it held fast. "Nobody got in here. Inside job—has to be. It's that Jo, all right. But I'll get it back."

"Ha!" The stranger burst into a mirthless laugh. "I'll believe that when I see it."

"Give me time!" Sidney left the sliding door and pounded toward the front end of the room, closely followed by McElroy.

They were leaving! Jo would have a chance now to look for another TRANSMUTER—if she dared to stay there, with Sidney so angry. He knew the Trick was gone, and he'd almost certainly return to make a search himself. But that was what she'd come for, and that was what she'd do. She flattened herself into the far corner while the men strode to the front of the room, bounded up the three steps, dashed through the narrow door, and banged it shut. She heard the click of its latch, and another click as the key turned in the lock. She was alone.

The Icy Pacific

JO STOOD IN THE REAR CORNER WITH HER hands clenched, trying to keep calm. She wanted to pound and yell for help, but she wouldn't, of course. She'd search for another TRANSMUTER as fast as she could, so she'd be ready to slip out again the minute someone opened the door. Maybe Mr. Paisley himself woud need one of his professional devices. And if he didn't, if Sid came instead, she'd keep quiet, and follow him out. "So get busy, Jo!" she said half aloud. "Find what you need! Quick!"

Even though she knew it was useless, she ran at once to the rolltop desk and opened all its drawers.

Nothing. She poked at the rear partition of the bottom drawer on the left, the short one, and took out its secret section. Empty. She removed all the other drawers again and measured them with her fingers. They were full-size. She felt every pigeonhole. They all contained only dust.

But the room held other hiding places, too, and she wasn't going to leave a single one untouched. Laying her backpack on the desk where she could find it again, she started to look through the large, complicated devices—trunks with secret escapes, chests to be sawed in half, vanishers to make things seem to disappear. *Seem* to! she wryly thought, as she lifted the nearest cover. They were kid stuff, compared to TRANSMUTER.

After searching these, she moved to the flimsy Capricorn tricks, and then to the furniture, pulling out cushions from chairs and sofas and running her hands into dusty crevices. Hurry, hurry, she kept telling herself, as she rushed from one piece to the next, but found nothing that could be of the slightest help.

When she was through, she dropped onto the green plush sofa and sat with her head in her hands, staring at the floor. She'd searched every shelf and every bit of furniture. Maybe there wasn't another TRANSMUTER, anywhere in the whole world! Or anything that would give her even a scrap of help. And she'd been in this room so long. Had Mr. Paisley left the Cave for the entire afternoon? Wasn't Sidney coming back?

As she sat there, looking vaguely at the floor, she noticed a shiny blue article, half-hidden under the edge of an overstuffed chair, and it reminded her that Sidney had found something in the desk and tossed it away. Was this it? Could it be of any use? With a tiny surge of hope, she picked it up and found that it was a common, small, spiral-bound notebook with a cardboard cover, the kind that could be bought in almost any grocery store. In the upper corner, in heavy, backhand writing was written "Henry Blake"; but Jo's spirits sagged again as she flipped it through, for it contained only page after page of lists, beginning:

Jan. 4   4 Thumb Tips, plastic. Engleburg Outfitters.   4/3.00
Jan. 9   6 pr. Loaded Dice   "   "   6/2.00

Nothing much, after all. And still—this shabby little book had belonged to Henry Blake, so Jo decided to take it home for Woody to see.

Woody! She jumped up. She couldn't tell time by her invisible watch, but it must be getting late! If Woody came home and found her room empty, he might start a search, and she'd be in a barrel of trouble then. She had to get out—but how? Everything here was solid, walls built of boards that would hold up a fort, floor vibrating with the waves, but well-built and sound. Even the small windows, two on each side wall, were so high they almost touched the ceiling, and they were protected by heavy black crossbars. Nothing moved except specks of dust, dancing in the sunbeams that slanted down through the dusty glass.

Could she climb through one of those? Although there was no ladder in sight, she might be able to stand on the rolltop desk, or build a tower of tables and chairs. But they were so high—and even if she somehow managed to reach them, how could she squeeze through the bars, or get down on the outside? It was too far to jump, and besides, she was invisible. She imagined herself falling and lying on the ground, injured, while people stumbled over her; or clinging to the window ledge and hollering, while people below stared without seeing her and wondered where the voice was coming from.

Could she throw out a message tied to a rock, as people did in books? "Help! I'm imprisoned! Let me out!" No better. That would alert the whole town, Mrs. Forbes included.

She stood up and walked around the edges of the room, poking and shoving, looking for a loose board, but the only moveable thing she could find was the sliding door at the rear, the one Sidney had tried to shake. Looking it over, she found that it was half the width of the wall, and hanging from a metal track. It was also very strong, being braced with rusty metal bands and fastened by three massive iron hooks, one waist high, one close to the floor, and one above her head. When Jo tried to shake it, it didn't budge. But maybe, if she could loosen the hooks ... Yes, if she did that, she could shove the door aside and swim to shore.

She took hold of the middle hook, which was as thick as her thumb, with its end bent down and wedged into a metal ring. It refused to move. She stood above it and lifted with all her strength. It was as unyielding as a cement seawall. Bracing her feet and setting her shoulder against it, she shoved the door toward the ring, in hope she could loosen it and flip it out. It didn't wiggle. She put the heel of her hand underneath, to give it a thrust. And at this the hook scraped upward by a hair's breadth.

Progress—at least a little! Jo thought, as she braced her hand again and shoved hard, ignoring the splinters. The hook moved another minute amount. She rested—shoved—rested—tried again—until all of a sudden the hook popped out with a clank. Startled, Jo turned and watched the narrow door, but neither Sidney nor Mr. Paisley appeared. She relaxed and turned back. She'd made a start.

The lower hook, which she tackled next, was wedged just as tightly as the other, and it was fastened so close to the floor that even when Jo knelt, she couldn't get her hand underneath to push it up. She curled her fingers around it and pulled until her wrist ached, without advancing it by so much as a millimeter. Could she put something under it, and pry it loose?

After looking through the boxes for a tool, she took a flimsy piece of rope from a Capricorn trick, slid it around the hook, gave it a sharp tug—and it broke. But her sneakers had laces that were almost new. Would they be strong enough?

Now keep your head! she told herself, as she sat down on the floor. With shaking fingers she pulled the laces out and doubled them into a stout cord, being extra careful not to drop them, because invisible laces would be hard to find. Slowly, awkwardly, unable to see what she was doing, she slipped the cord around the shank of the hook, looped it around her hand, and got to her knees in order to give it a sharp tug. It moved—or seemed to. Another tug—it moved some more. And at her next pull, it slipped all the way out of the iron ring. Only one was left.

However, this was so high that even when she stretched, Jo could barely touch it with the tip of her fingers. But she knew how to dislodge the hooks now, so she ran in her bare feet to the clutter of furniture and brought back a chair. When she climbed on this, she was able to push with the heel of her hand, as she had before, so she braced herself and shoved until the hook popped out. She'd released them all!

As soon as Jo had caught her breath, she tugged the heavy door open a crack, just to make sure she really could, and closed it immediately, for fear someone in a boat might see it and alert Mr. Paisley. Remembering how rocky the shore was, she put on her sneakers, untwisted the laces, and tied them well. Since she still had the empty sandwich bag, she stuffed the notebook into that and returned it to her pocket. It showed against her invisible self, but she left it there, because she had no other way to carry it home. And then, ready at last, she zipped up her jacket, put on her backpack, and opened the door just wide enough to slip through, closing it at once.

The sun was bright and seagulls were soaring overhead, as Jo stood on the wide deck which reached across the Cave and Sky High, but not across the Surf Riders' store on one side, or Davy Jones's Chowder House on the other. Since the Surf Riders' was smaller, she decided to swim around that one, and then alongside it to shore.

She hesitated for a minute, looking down at the waves, which were still high from the storm of the day before, slapping against the timbers. They were steely blue, with green and black shadows in their troughs, and Jo shivered at the thought of jumping in; for even in summer the Pacific was cold, and this was early spring. But she had no choice, so she drew a deep breath, sat down at the edge of the deck, and slid off feet first.

It was like plunging through a pack of ice cubes. The water stung her, closed over her head, made her gasp. Without reaching bottom, she kicked hard, fought her way to the surface and gulped for air, then started a slow, even crawl among the wooden piles.

For the first few strokes she watched the waves churning around her invisible feet, while her body created a blank cylindrical space and her hands scooped out empty troughs. She could see the notebook swimming along as if it were a little square fish on an errand of its own. But she knew that no one could last long in water as cold as this, so she lowered her head and put all her strength into swimming, not trying to hurry, saving her strength. If she got into trouble, nobody could see her to offer help.

Waves lifted and lowered her as she glided under the deck of the Cave and Sky High, and then toward the end of the Surf Riders' shop. She was tossed hard against a piling, which bruised her shoulder and cost her a stroke; but she forged grimly on to the end of the building, where she turned toward shore. When she saw boulders just ahead, she moved more slowly, alert for the first sharp touch. Here it was, an underwater rock that clawed at her fingers and gouged her knee, stinging, although she couldn't see any blood. She bumped into another rock, set her hand against it, and steadied herself with both arms while she waited for a trough between waves. When a broad one came, she scrambled to the stony bank, and she was safe.

She was also dripping wet, shivering, and facing a long walk home. Should she go to the Jolly Rodgers? And dribble water all over the floor, while her disembodied voice explained her predicament? Never! she thought. Mrs. Forbes would either holler her head off and run for help, or take Jo to the hospital and send for her parents. Cold as she was, she'd walk home by herself.

But she had to do something about the notebook before someone saw it. Crouching on the rocks beside the bay, and keeping close to the ground, Jo slid it out of the sandwich bag, which had leaked a lot. However, a hasty glance told her that the writing was still legible, so she gave it a shake and threw it up the bank, as she would skip a stone, then scrambled to her feet and started after it.

Shivering, kicking the notebook ahead of her with unobtrusive, small jerks, Jo trudged along Old Main Street. With her first steps, she noticed that the water trickling from her clothes left a trail of footprints. She stepped into the gutter, and managed to shove the notebook there, too. Now, however, the drifts of sand that had blown up from the beach squished under her feet, leaving dents that changed shape with every step—a giveaway, if anyone happened to look. After a few steps, she moved cautiously onto the sidewalk again, and since her clothes were no longer dripping enough to leave a trail, she went on as fast as she could, walking—jogging—walking—nudging the notebook ahead of her. Although this end of the street was nearly deserted, she met a young women pushing a stroller, followed by a little girl on roller skates, and she moved out of their way.

At the first corner she turned and took the back streets home, sneakers squelching on the walk. Before she had gone far, some boys came along, riding sideways on skateboards, with their knees bent and wheels humming beneath them. One of them swooped to a stop and picked up the notebook. "Hey, it's wet!" he exclaimed, as he leafed through it. "Nah!" he said when he was through, and hurled it far ahead.

At least, Jo thought, he sent it in the right direction, which would help some. As soon as the boys had rolled away, she found the notebook and nudged it back onto the sidewalk, where she continued to kick it along.

Although the sun was bright, a cold wind was blowing across her wet hair and sopping clothes, and she shivered. The climb was long and steep, and she felt as if every muscle in her body had turned to a chunk of ice. She had six blocks left—

five—four. Close to home, she met Domino again, and as before, he sniffed at her heels, sat down and howled, then scuttled away.

She was nearly home now—and she was frozen! She had to get there and get warm again, before she turned into an absolute icicle. Snatching up the notebook and recklessly letting it show, she tore around the house into the backyard, snatched the key from its hidden nail, and went inside.

She raced upstairs and into the bathroom. Teeth chattering, she pulled off her clothes and turned on the hot water. No shower this time! She needed to soak! As soon as the tub was a third full, she climbed in, but didn't turn off the faucet until she was covered almost to her neck. The water looked peculiar, with a hollow space molded to her invisible shape—but it felt heavenly! She'd stay in it for a long time!

Slowly, as the wonderful warmth crept into her bones, she stopped shivering, and at last she climbed out and put a Band-Aid on the sticky place where her knee had been scraped. The Band-Aid showed, but nobody was there to see it.

After dressing in dry clothes, she wrung out her invisible ones as best she could and carried them to her room, to hang them in the closet and hope they wouldn't drip too much. Right now, without wasting a second, she'd get started with that Capricorn notebook. She put a sheet of paper on a clipboard, but she was tired, so tired that she left the chair to curl up under a blanket on her bed, where she could work and keep warm at the same time. "Thumb Tips," the notebook said. "Loaded Dice."

Jo started to make a list. *Thumb Tips* . . . But the pencil fell from her hand, and she slid farther down under the blanket. She was asleep.

We'll Try Them All

WHEN JO WOKE UP, THE LATE AFTERNOON SUN was slanting through her window, and she could hear Woody and Mrs. Forbes talking downstairs. Were they at dinner? Jo wondered, catching a whiff of the smell from below. Mrs. Forbes's meat loaf, she thought, perhaps cooked until it was dry—but her stomach felt absolutely hollow. As soon as the coast was clear, she'd creep into the kitchen and see what she could find—an apple, or some cookies and a glass of milk. Imagining she had them already on her desk, she closed her eyes again and drifted into another nap.

A stealthy tapping awakened her. "Hey, Jo, it's

145

me," said Woody's voice, and when she opened the door, he was standing there with a tray in his hand.

"Hungry?" he asked, kicking the door shut with his foot.

"Starved!" Jo scraped some papers aside, making room on her desk for the tray. "Meat loaf. Milk. Cookies. Two oranges! Woody—*thanks*!" She sat down and took her first bite.

"Boy, it sure is funny, seeing your clothes sit there all by themselves, and your fork sailing up and down," said Woody, as he dropped onto the floor and peeled an orange. "Your show would be a winner if you could do this in public."

"And get myself into a mess."

"Maybe not. You could be the Transparent Lady. She has a Voice. She Can Move Things. But You Can't See Her. Step right up, folks. ..." Turning serious, he jerked his head toward the notepaper lying on her bed. "You must have found something. Treasure?"

"Hardly. Just a dumb little notebook. I was trying to figure it out, and I went to sleep."

Woody picked up her notes and gave them a quick glance. "Hmm. Not much so far," he agreed. "But tell me about it. Forbes is lost in the tube, so she won't even think about us for a while."

"Well ..." Jo began. "I got into the back room all right, because Sid showed it to a stranger. That much was easy. It turned out that Sidney knew about TRANSMUTER, and—Woody, he was planning to sell it to that man! Behind Mr. Paisley's back." She paused, expecting Woody to remind her of the way she had gotten the trick, but he only sat up straighter and stared in her direction.

"Hey! Maybe Sid knows the code," he exclaimed.

"Not a chance. He said he's never worked it, not even once. But he found out Transmuter was gone, and—Woody, he's figured out that I have it!" She repeated all that had happened. "It's a good thing I can swim," she finished.

"Hmm! Have to hand it to you. That wasn't exactly recreation." Woody finished peeling his orange and tossed the rinds into the wastebasket. "And now let's see where we stand. Did you hear anything that might help?" He took a pen and notepad out of his pocket.

"Not a word. But I found this, and I was trying to make sense of it when I went to sleep." Jo groped for the notebook, found it under the edge of the blanket, and handed it over. "I think it's lists of supplies. And I had an awful time getting it home, because it's visible. So I kicked it along."

Grinning, Woody thumbed through the wet pages. "It swam in, too, I can see that. Where'd it come from?"

"Sidney found it in the desk and threw it away." She explained what had happened, while Woody ran his finger down the first page.

"What's Engleburg? Ever heard of it?" he asked.

"It's a supply house. I saw their catalog once," Jo replied. "Honest, Woody, I don't think this silly little book will be any help."

"We'll try, anyway. At least we can eliminate an awful lot of these entries. If you think the last two letters of your code are violet, indigo . . ."

"I don't think. I know."

"Okay." Woody was thumbing through the notebook. "Anyway, that means the last two letters of the long word are the same as the first two letters of a short one. The one that's repeated four times. So we can scratch off stuff like Linking Rings, because those last letters are *g-s*—and that doesn't begin a three-letter word. Get it?"

"I think so." Jo felt doubtful.

"And your control box has only seven colors, so we can't have more than seven different letters. See?"

"It sounds complicated."

"Not too bad. Actually, it saves a lot of time. So let's get moving." Woody turned to the first page. "Thumb Tips—that ends with *ps*, which doesn't start a three-letter word, so it's wrong. Loaded Dice? Same."

They worked their way down the scribbled lists. Melville the Dragon was out—too many different letters. So were Turkish Tops and Wiley Williard. Eureka Cat was only seven different letters, but when they tried it with the control box, it didn't bring Jo back, and neither did Fantastica.

An hour and a half later, Woody tossed the note-book onto the desk. "Zilch. I'm afraid it's a dud, sis. Sorry about that." Bony, long-legged, still sprawled on the floor, he buried his face in his hands. "Seems as if we should be able to do it, though. This was invented by a person, just a common, ordinary person, and a person ought to be able to figure it out."

Jo, at the desk, rummaged through their papers, while an idea knocked at her, demanding to be heard. She couldn't quite place it. Four? Something about that? "Woody?" she ventured. "Why is that first word—violet, indigo, blue—repeated four times? Does it mean something that has to do with four? Like four-wheeler? What else come in fours? Quartets? Four seasons?"

"Hey!" Woody sat up straight, his eyes bright again. "You have an idea there! Four horsemen?"

"Four quarters." Jo reached for the books that were standing on her desk. "Here's my dictionary. If we can't find the right one in this, we could use the unabridged from downstairs."

They sat side by side on the bed with the dictionary between them, opened to "four."

"Wow! What a lot," Woody exclaimed in a few minutes. "Four-cycle—eight different letters—too many. Four-flush . . ." He counted them. "Seven different letters. *Sh* could be the beginning of 'she,' but then *e* would be the eighth letter, and that's too many. Four-footed—nope. Its last two letters don't start a three-letter word. Four Freedoms—eight different letters." He glanced up, because Jo had thrown her pencil and paper onto the floor. "Hey, don't stop now. We're just beginning."

Jo bristled. Woody, bright-eyed and eager, was playing a game again, as if he had a brand-new computer! He ought to try sneaking through doors, struggling into clothes he couldn't see, dodging people, swimming in that icy water! And then, as she thought of his efforts to help, her anger melted away, and she picked up her paper again.

She read off words while he jotted them down. They listed four-handed, Four Hundred, four-masted, four-o'clock, fourpence, fourscore, foursome and foursquare. None of them worked.

Discouraged, Jo looked again toward the dictionary page. "The trouble is, they don't make sense. Quartet. Seasons. Horsemen. I should think the word would have something to do with vanishing. Maybe ... here are some that start with 'fourth.' Fourth-class ..." She counted. "Too many letters. But fourth dimension. Dimension!" She shoved back her chair and leaped to her feet. "*Dimension!* Woody! Fourth Dimension! Could *disappearing* have something to do with being in a *dimension*? If it does, then ..."

"Hey!" Woody scrambled to his feet and ran his hand through his hair, making it stand straight up. "Fourth dimension—that's a lot of letters. But dimension by itself! Two ... three ... seven! Let's give it a try! Quick! Some bigger paper." Jo handed him several sheets and a clipboard from her desk drawer, and he flopped onto the floor, scribbling as he talked.

"*Dimension.* That's the best idea yet. We'll put its letters over what few colors we know, and see how they look." He was muttering under his breath. "Violet, indigo, blue. That's the short word. Don't bother with it now. Start with green, yellow, orange. And those—if we're lucky—will stand for the first three letters of 'dimension.' Like this." He held a sheet of paper toward Jo. "Are you there? You try it, too."

Jo plopped onto the bed, with her feet tucked under her, and for a moment the code was exciting, like a game of Clue. She braced her elbow against a stuffed kangaroo and started to write, saying the letters aloud.

"*D - i - m.* Green, yellow, orange. Leave a lot of room in the middle, and end with *o - n.* That's violet, indigo. . . . Careful now. We don't want to . . ."

"And you might just simmer down," Woody muttered. "I'm trying to think."

"Oh, sorry."

Jo wrote the rest of the word and added what colors she knew. "Like this?" she asked, turning her page toward her brother.

D	I	M	E	N	S	I	O	N
GREEN YELLOW ORANGE			—	—	—	—	VIOLET INDIGO	

"That's right," he said. "And the *n* in the middle has to be indigo, same as the one on the end. And the second *i*—that's yellow. Same as the other."

Jo filled it in. Her paper now said:

D	I	M	E	N	S	I	O	N
GREEN	YELLOW	ORANGE	—	INDIGO	—	YELLOW	VIOLET	INDIGO

"Let's have a look," said Woody, when she finished. "Yep. We match."

Jo drew a deep breath.

"Now, if 'dimension' is the right word, then violet, indigo is *o-n*," said Woody, scribbling again. "We'll use that for the short word that's repeated four times, so put it in now, on a separate line. And the only three-letter word I can think of that starts with *o-n* is 'one.' So, if violet-indigo-blue is *o-n*-blank, then the blue has to be *e*."

"Violet, indigo, blue ... *o - n - e*."

"That's right. Fill it in. And that means the *e* in 'dimension' is blue."

Jo's heart was beating fast as she added the new section

O	N	E
VIOLET	INDIGO	BLUE *(four times)*

D	I	M	E	N	S	I	O	N
GREEN	YELLOW	ORANGE	BLUE	INDIGO	—	YELLOW	VIOLET	INDIGO

"And the only color left is red for the *s*," Woody said next.

"That's all!" Jo felt as one more breath might be her last. "I ... I ... Woody! Suppose we're wrong!"

Woody was sober. "Then we try some of those other words. But this looks reasonable." He scribbled "red" into its place under the *s*. "So here it is. The whole thing! Is it like yours?"

They laid their papers side by side, and found that each had written:

O   N   E

VIOLET   INDIGO   BLUE   *(four times)*

D   I   M   E   N   S   I   O   N

GREEN YELLOW ORANGE BLUE INDIGO   RED YELLOW VIOLET INDIGO

They matched.

"Have you got the box?" Woody asked.

"Do you think I'd lose *that*?" Jo reached into the drawer for the leather case, which still contained the invisible parts of TRANSMUTER.

Woody rolled his eyes, and watched the case apparently float through the air, but for once he didn't mention it. Instead, his voice was solemn as he said, "Good. Give it a try."

Trembling, Jo took out the parts of the Trick, laid the shawl on the bed, and sat down at the desk with the control box in her hands. She turned it and turned it again, groping for the buttons, making sure the row of them was on top, the single one underneath. It felt the same as always—cool, hard-edged, with the knobby buttons standing up like those on a calculator. Maybe they'd solved it. Maybe in a few seconds she'd be herself again. She must be careful now, and not make a mistake. Biting her lip in concentration, she began.

Violet—button number one. Indigo—number two. Blue—number three. Do those four times. This much seemed familiar.

Green, yellow, orange—four, five, and six. And then she worked with extreme caution, saying the words out loud and counting each button, while Woody pointed along the line, color by color. Blue—third button from the left. Violet—the first. Red—the sixth ... no, orange was number six! She counted it twice, to be sure. Red had to be seven, next to black, which was on the end. Yellow—number five again. And then violet, indigo—easy ones—and she was through.

But nothing happened.

"Wrong ... word." Woody's voice sounded hollow and slow, as if it came through a long, vast, echoing pipe. "Well—tough luck, sis." Shaking his head, he stared at the list of colors. "But all is not lost. We'll try another."

"Maybe ... maybe ..." Jo faltered. It couldn't, *couldn't* be! Their plan, their wonderful plan, *couldn't* turn out to be a flop! And she suddenly remembered. "Woody! There's one more! The white button, on the back!"

"Well, let's have it!"

"Right."Jo felt the underside of the box, pressed the button—and still nothing happened. "I guess...we aren't as smart as we thought we were." She felt terrible, worse than when she was swimming through the icy water, worse than when Sidney locked her in.

"Never mind. We've got plenty more ideas," Woody stoutly told her. "We'll try 'fourteen.' Or 'four score...'"

She couldn't bear it! Jo thought as she picked up her paper. She had been so sure! Blinking back tears, she ran her fingers again over the sharp-edged keys. She turned the box around from left to right—and back again—and either way, it felt the same. Was *that* what was wrong? "Woody! *Listen!* Suppose I'm holding the box backwards! The buttons are right in the middle. So, if I have it reversed—that would put black on the left instead of violet. Woody! Do you suppose...Shall I try it over?"

"Hey! I *guess!*"

"Let's see, now. I turned it once, and turned it back, so it's the same way I've already tried. I'll turn it once more...." Although Jo couldn't see the box, she could feel it well, and she carefully turned it around. "Here goes!" she whispered, and started to repeat the routine, with Woody leaning toward her and reading the colors as before.

She counted every button and counted it again, before pressing it. "Woody—I'm scared. I think I did them right, but . . ." She lifted the box, felt for the button on the bottom, and held her breath as she pressed it. White.

How Scared, How Brave, is Jo?

JO FELT HERSELF PLUNGE! IT WAS AS IF A featherbed plopped on top of her, not sharp, not hard, not heavy, yet shoving her flat against the bed, weighing her down and shutting off her breath. She gasped. The room swayed. The bed rocked. The fir branches outside the window billowed, and so did the silver-gray window frame. Even Woody's beaming face wavered back and forth, split by a broad grin, with his teeth showing white.

He was yelling at her. "Hey, sis! *I can see you! You're all there!* We *did* it!" He pounded her arm, shook her knee, and patted her head so vehemently that it bobbed on the pillow. "The shawl's here, too—directions—control box."

157

"Good!" Jo struggled to sit up straight, but her legs and arms felt tied down and her head was almost too heavy to lift. "We won't ever forget that again!"

"I guess not!" Woody jumped up and grabbed the box, looking it over—top, bottom, and all sides. "Pretty neat, all right. How does it feel, anyway, to be back on earth?"

"Like weighing a ton," Jo told him. "But I'm better already. Things have almost quit spinning." She lifted a hand, lifted a foot, and found they worked exactly as they always had.

"Well, I 'spect it's quite a shock. Being in Fourth Dimension—or whatever that was—probably makes you extra light, so you feel like a ton when you come back." He was holding the box in both hands. "Say, Jo, give me that shawl. I'd like to try ..."

"Woody! This isn't a toy."

But Woody insisted. "Who helped figure your trick out? Who brought you food? Who hasn't blabbed, not once, about what a mess you got into? Huh?"

"You. Of course."

"Then who deserves a turn better than I do? Huh?"

"Nobody. Of course." She reluctantly handed him the shawl and watched while he made all the stuffed animals invisible, then tried to toss them up into the air and catch them, sight unseen.

"What a blast!" he exclaimed, when he had brought them back. "Now I'm going to vanish myself."

"Woody! You're out of your mind! You *wouldn't*!"

"Wouldn't I not! My carcass belongs to me. I can mistreat it as much as I want."

"You won't like it ... but all right."

If Woody wanted to try being invisible, she guessed he had earned the right.

Grinning, eyes glittering behind the dark-rimmed glasses, he was already pressing buttons. Green. Yellow.... Black! And he was gone.

With invisible hands he picked up a book, and it floated through the air. "How *radical! Super!*" He slipped down the hall and came back wearing different jeans and T-shirt. "So's I can see my clothes standing up without me in them," he explained.

"Look! This isn't a joke! Maybe it feels like fun right now, but it isn't. I've been trapped in it, and I know." Jo paused. "I want another glass of milk and I've got to phone Kim. While I'm doing that, you play with the Trick, only *please* don't do anything awful."

"Sure," his voice replied, as a chair rose up and floated across the room.

While the furniture, pillows, books gyrated in the air, Jo perched on her desk chair to dial. "Kim— I'm all right!" she exclaimed when Kim answered.

"You're ... well again? Yourself?"

"As good as new." Jo told her about the swim, and solving the Trick. "Woody helped me. He's worked lots of codes," she finished. "Kim, can you come over first thing in the morning?"

"I'll be there, all right. I want to see you!" Kim exclaimed. "You must at least be goofy. Or weak. Or something."

"Goofy? Well, maybe." Jo giggled. "Honest, Kim, I'm fine. Not even a scar."

A few minutes later she went downstairs, reveling in the wonderful sight of her own feet moving up and down. She stopped in the doorway of the living room, where Mrs. Forbes was sitting on her favorite chair, knitting a red scarf and watching the tube. "Hi! I'm home!" Jo said.

"Why, Jo—when did you come in?" Mrs. Forbes asked without turning around. "I didn't hear you. Have you had dinner?"

"Oh, sure. I just got back." What would Mrs. Forbes say if she knew where Jo had really been? "I'm not hungry, but I'd like some milk."

"Of course, dear. It's nice to have you with us, but Woody and I did quite well by ourselves." Mrs. Forbes bent closer to the screen. "I think that handsome one is a spy," she said, and then added, "Did you and Kim have a good time?"

"It was ... incredible." And that was the literal truth, Jo thought. She heard a footstep, and knew Woody was in the room, invisible. "We tried, as *everyone* should, to show some common sense," she continued, raising her voice and looking toward the place where her brother must be. Was that cackling whisper a laugh? And the cushion! It rose up and turned around.

"Common sense? Oh, yes, that's very wise," Mrs. Forbes replied with a vague smile. "Such a foolish woman! Still in the office! While that fellow hangs around!" Shaking her head, she added, "Is your show going well? Is your act all worked out?"

"Not quite. But we have lots of ideas."

"Sensational ones! She showed them to me," Woody explained. Visible again, he was standing in the doorway, holding the little gray box.

"I'm sure you'll do well," Mrs. Forbes placidly replied, as Jo headed for the kitchen.

The next morning when Jo awoke, she waved an arm back and forth in the air, for the sheer pleasure of watching it move. She could see her wrist bending and turning—hand, fingers, even the fingernails, all solid and real. Rolling over, she poked a leg out from under the blanket and yes, it was visible, too, the same skinny foot as always, attached to the same bony ankle.

Duchess was on the bed, purring, and Jo stroked her under the chin. "I'm back! I'm *me, myself!* I can wear whatever I want to, and eat at the table, and take a walk without having a dog howl at me! While you, silly cat, don't seem to care. But that's okay. You've liked me all along."

It was early and the house was quiet, so Jo pulled

the blankets to her chin and closed her eyes. A great question was pounding through her mind. Should she use TRANSMUTER in the talent show? It would be scary to do it onstage; but if she could muster up that much courage, the act would be a sensation. They could vanish a chair—a big one that would show up well. Some silks—bright colored. Her magician's stand.

But the really stupendous climax, the sure-fire way to make a real impression, would be—herself! Could she risk it, with all those people watching— the dizzy whirl, the floor going up and down, the churned feeling in her stomach? Could she stand to look down and see the boards right through her shoes? She started to dress, trying to think it through.

Breakfast that morning was wonderful—Woody's pancakes, eaten while they were hot. Just after it was over and Mrs. Forbes had left for the shop, Kim burst through the door.

"Jo! Are you really okay?" she asked as they ran up the stairs. She stared at Jo, openmouthed, and added, "You're *you,* all right. You look just the same as always."

Jo laughed as they hurried into her room and closed the door. Everything today was perfect— funny—exciting. "Of course! I *am* the same as always."

"Not stiff or numb or anything?"

"Nothing. I feel marvelous." Jo spun on her heels so Kim could see her from all sides.

"Well, *that's* a relief!" Kim's shoulders heaved in a tremendous sigh. "You can get rid of that stupid Trick now, and not ever have to worry about it again."

"Get *rid* of it!" Jo stopped in the middle of a whirl. "Kim—I've just learned how to work it! I'm going to keep it forever! And maybe I'll use it in the talent show!"

"You *couldn't!*"

Jo thought about her life if she gave up the Trick—safe and serene, also dull. But if she kept TRANSMUTER, she could put on an act such as Madrona had never seen before. She might become famous! For years and years she had wanted to be a second Siegfried, and this was her big chance. "You know, I've had a pretty hard time," she said, keeping her voice calm, because Kim was perched on the edge of the bed with her hands braced, as if she might leap off and run straight out the door.

"You're not the only one. I've had a hard time, too."

"Sure. But I learned a lot, and I'd like to make use of it. We could knock folks right out of their seats. We could vanish a chair. And some silks. And then . . ." Jo stopped. Was it right to put TRANSMUTER on a public stage, where the wrong kind of person might see it and get hold of it and use it the wrong

way? And what about Sidney, who already sus-
pected that she had it? If he saw it in the show,
he'd be sure. Did she dare do it in front of him?

Jo set her jaw. Of course she dared! She'd watch
TRANSMUTER every second, to keep it safe. Sidney
was just the long-legged tease who ran Sky High,
and that man with the bossy voice had gone. She'd
never have such a chance again, so—yes! She'd
try! "And then—me!" she exclaimed.

Kim jumped up as if she had been struck. "You!
You're off your rocker. Make *yourself* disappear?
On the *stage*? That's the lousiest idea I ever heard."

"Not *lousy*! It'll be a sensation,"

"It *stinks*!"

"The audience won't think so."

"It's too *scary*! Remember the mess you were in?
Suppose you lose the directions again!" Kim's high
voice was higher still.

"Lose the directions?" Jo shrugged. "What of it?
I know the code word now, so I could easily figure
it out. And Kim, I'll be the one to say the patter and
keep the act going. All you have to do is press the
buttons."

"*Me!* Press those awful *buttons*! After what *happened*! Jo, I couldn't! Suppose I make a mistake!
Or drop the box!" Slinging her jeans bag over her
shoulder, Kim moved toward the door.

Jo looked at the posters of Houdini, David Copperfield, Siegfried and Roy. Some day, maybe, she

could be as famous as they were—and she'd never know unless she tried. "I really want to do it, and we're a team," she pleaded. "I suppose I could get another partner, but ... please. I'll do the hard part."

"Uh-uh."

"I don't want to tell anyone else what TRANSMUTER is. I need you."

"Well ..." Kim hesistated. "All right. I'll try. But you've got to show at least a little sense."

"Oh, I will. You won't be sorry. And Kim, thanks. It ... well ... I'm really glad." Jo took her card table and magician stand out of the closet and set them up in the front room, ready to practice.

They started by checking the props and running through their old acts, after which Jo gathered up the silks from all of her unused tricks and stuffed them into a discarded percolator, on top of a collapsible white dove.

"I'll pull them out—and make them disappear," she said.

"Jo, the Zombie Balls, the ones your dad gave you, are really good, and you've nearly learned them," Kim timidly suggested. "I know you could do them. Shall we try?"

Jo considered. With the aid of a wire gimmick, the Balls were supposed to float above a cloth. Only a few weeks ago she had almost mastered them. But now ... "No—I haven't time for new things," she replied. "Our act is going so well, let's not change it."

"Oh, okay." They began their routine.

After Kim left at noon, Jo intended to walk down the long hill to Old Town, to take her turn at the Jolly Rodgers. But before starting, she glanced out of the window and saw the gray car parked at the nearest corner, with the stranger at the wheel and Sidney beside him. "Not *them!*" she gasped. She ran back to her room, vanished the Trick, rolled the leather case into her sleeping bag, and put the control box and shawl into her largest hiking boots. She laid these on the top shelf of her closet, behind a stack of boxes, and then slipped out the back door, where Sidney couldn't see her go.

She went to town by a different route than usual, and when she returned at dinnertime, she found her boots and sleeping bag untouched. "But from now on I'll keep the Trick hidden except when I'm using it," she said to Woody.

"Good idea," he agreed.

The next day, while Woody was at the Jolly Rodgers, Jo and Kim practiced again, and Kim suggested using the Journey Through Space. "My birthday present, but I can't do it very well," she said. "You could, though."

"I know it's good, Kim—but we don't need it."

"It's really interesting," Kim insisted.

"Sure, some other time. Transmuter—that's our big thing. Let's try it right now." Jo's mouth felt dry as she picked up the shawl, and she could see Kim's hands trembling on the control box.

The first part was easy. Jo chanted an antique spell and closed her eyes for a few seconds, while the room spun around her. Things soon settled down, and she twirled the rope and elevated a chair and card table, as they had planned. When it was time to become visible again, she clutched her stand with both hands and braced herself. "Here goes," she said.

"I don't *like* this!" Kim exclaimed, fingers on the buttons.

"I'm okay." Jo held fast and started a longer spell. "Abac. Aldal. Hibac. Guthac. Guthor. Elemiath. Tetrogrammaton. Ready? Is your finger on white?"

Kim nodded.

"Now, the last word. *Tzaphniel!*"

There it was—the jolt, the dizzy sweep of the floor—just as before, while everything in sight— pictures on the walls, bookcases, lamps, wood- work—stretched sideways into long, blurred streaks. Why did I try it? Jo asked herself, as she closed her eyes and clung tightly to her stand; and even this, hard and angular, seemed to float up and down, pulling at her arms. But things slowly turned steady again. She managed to stay on her feet, and when she opened her eyes, she decided it hadn't been so bad after all. "I can do it," she said. "I know what to expect now, and that helps."

"It gives me the willies," Kim told her.

"But it's a good act! The audience will like it."
As they were putting their equipment away, Jo
glanced out of the window. "Kim—he's there, coming up the walk."

"Who?" asked Kim, standing beside her.

"Sidney—that creep. At least he's alone this
time." Jo dodged back from the window. "S-s-sh!
Don't let him know we're here."

A moment later the doorbell rang, but the girls
waited out of sight until they heard footsteps leaving the porch. When they looked out again, Sidney
had left.

At their next practice, on Thursday morning,
everything went wrong. They hadn't packed the
drum properly, so its dolls were stuck. Kim mis-
placed the percolator full of silks. Going invisible
was a jolt, and when Jo turned herself visible again,
she lost her balance and dropped flat on the floor.
For once she was relieved to turn her back on
magic and set out for the Jolly Rodgers, leaving
TRANSMUTER hidden as before, while Woody re-
mained at home.

It was a rainy day. Jo's feet were wet by the time
she got to town. The shop was chilly, and few shoppers appeared. She was counting the minutes until
closing when Woody suddenly charged in, shouting, "Jo! Mrs. Forbes! Are you all right?"

"Of course." Mrs. Forbes came forward in her
teetery shoes. "Has something happened?"

Woody stared at them. "Who telephoned?"

"Telephoned? Not I!" Mrs. Forbes turned around. "Jo, dear, did you call Woody?"

"Nope." A cold hand seemed to clutch Jo's stomach. "Woody—what is it?"

"Telephone call." He was still breathing hard. "A man said I was needed at the shop, and hung up. I thought sure there was a fire or something, so I came on my bike."

"He wanted you out of the house!" Setting down a brass lamp, Jo raced toward the door. TRANSMU-TER! Even though it was invisible, anybody who really searched might thrust a hand into the boot and feel the control box and shawl. She must hurry—hurry—and find out whether they were safe!

"I'll take you home, Woody." Mrs. Forbes was already walking toward the back of the store. "Jo, you stay here to tend the shop, while we ..."

"I'm coming along," Jo insisted, and a moment later, with the shop temporarily locked, they were all three in the station wagon, on their way up the hill.

As soon as Mrs. Forbes stopped in front of their house, Woody and Jo leaped out and dashed into the front hall, just in time to hear the slam of the kitchen door. Running outside, they saw someone scuttling away but he was so far off and moved so fast that they couldn't tell who it was.

They tore into the house and upstairs to Jo's room, where they stopped in dismay because clothes and shoes, books and papers were strewn across the entire floor. Drawers had been dumped, clothes pulled off their hangers, the desk rifled.

Jo's heart was hammering as she charged across the mess, groped on the closet shelf, and—yes, the boots were just where she had left them, behind the last stack of boxes. She plunged in her hand and felt the shawl and control box still there, still invisible. "I guess we scared him off in time!" she said, running her fingers along the buttons, which flipped up and down in their usual crisp way. "It's a good thing you hurried, Woody."

"Yeah. But boy, was I taken in! Talk about dummies! Me! Mr. Cool! I panicked! Didn't even have the brains to stay here and telephone the shop."

"Is there trouble?" called Mrs. Forbes, climbing the stairs.

"I think—someone's been in here," Jo replied.

"Oh, *dear*! What a dreadful sight!" Mrs. Forbes was standing in the doorway. "I'll cable your parents at once. Although . . ."

"No need for that. Everything's okay," Jo hastily said. "It's messed up, that's all. I can straighten it out in no time. And *please* don't bother Mom and Dad. It'd ruin their trip."

"Well, if you're sure . . ." Mrs. Forbes picked up a skirt and shook it out. "If nothing's gone . . ."

"It's okay," Jo repeated.

"Sure it is," Woody agreed. When Mrs. Forbes had started downstairs, he added to Jo, "We'd better keep the Trick in my room after this. Nobody'd find it in the middle of my electrical gear."

"Good." Jo felt reassured.

That evening she collected the parts of TRANS-MUTER and took them to Woody, to be kept among his electronic equipment. Before going to bed she locked her window; and in the night, when she opened it to let Duchess in, she looked out. Was that a dark form hovering in the shadows of the backyard? She couldn't quite see. But she was frightened, even though the Trick was probably safe, invisible and stored among Woody's clutter.

And then it was Friday, the day of the show.

Jo was up early, rereading their list of props and making sure they were all packed.

"Hi, everybody! We're going to ..." She ran through the patter.

She tried to read, and laid down her book when she realized that she'd gone over the same page three times and still didn't know what it said.

She washed her hair and pressed her magician's cloak.

At dinner, she only picked at the food. "No, no more, really," she insisted when Mrs. Forbes urged her to take a second helping. "I'm just ... not hungry!"

She raced up to her room. Her shirt, her shoes, her pants. She had them on. Her wand—packed. Her case of props—loaded. TRANSMUTER—safely among the props, and she'd hang on to it every second of the show. *Why didn't Mrs. Forbes hurry?*

"I'll see you in the car!" called Woody, banging on her door.

And at last Jo heard Mrs. Forbes's voice. "Jo! It's time to leave! Are you ready?"

"Ready! I've been waiting for ages!" Jo came tumbling downstairs, wrapped in her black cloak. She was on the way.

Joanna Rodgers, Magician

THE TALENT SHOW WAS LIKE THE TRYOUT, YET it was different. The stage was larger, the backstage larger, and most of the performers were in high school instead of junior high. Jo sat on a folding chair with one hand on the suitcase that contained TRANSMUTER, not letting go for an instant. While she waited through an endless skit, a gymnast, a dancer, and a pair of singers, she reassured Kim, who was standing up and sitting down, smoothing her pink skirt, poking at her hair.

"*Good* evening, everybody. How about ..." Still keeping her hand on the case, Jo murmured patter under her breath, practiced deep breathing, straightened her tie. But when at last it was her turn, she felt quite calm as she helped the stage-hands arrange their props. The curtains opened. And the two girls stepped onto the stage.

Jo had decided to start straight, as she had in the tryout, switch to the comic role that had been so popular, and then, when the audience least expected a surprise, to introduce the Trick.

"I've brought some peculiar rings!" she exclaimed, remembering to speak clearly, even though this auditorium had stage microphones. "Do they link themselves? Or do they ..."

The stunt with Rings went without a hitch, as did the one with Al the Alligator, while the audience watched—not excited, but friendly and attentive, just as Jo had hoped.

Her next act was the Growth Accelerator, for which she neglected to press the button, as before. But this time it was intentional, and the audience seemed to be expecting it, for they broke into laughter the instant the rabbit appeared, limp and dangling in her hand.

She dropped the Unbeatable Drum and tossed the paper-flat dolls into the air, while the laughter increased. She shook out a blue silk, poked it into her hand, lighted the match—and brought it out with the charred, brown hole. "Aw-w-wful!" She put her finger into her mouth and rolled her eyes, while the audience tittered.

Picking up the rabbit again, she let it hang, pretended to cry, and wiped her eyes with its ears. So far it was going just as she had planned, and the laughter became a roar.

And then it was time for the new part of the act. "I'm tired!" She lowered her voice to a groan. "Frazzled. Tuckered out. I need to sit down."

"Maybe—on this?" Although Kim had so far been pink-cheeked and smiling, she turned pale and her voice quavered as she brought over a folding chair.

"It's all right!" Jo whispered. "Everything's fine."

She lowered herself onto the chair, but immediately bounced to her feet and turned around to glare at it. "Too hard! Let's *eradicate it*! With a magic spell!" Heart beating fast, she draped the shawl on the chair, not letting it touch anything else. She tiptoed around it in a circle, picked up her wand, and held it high above her head as she chanted. "Abac. Aldal. Hibac. Guthac. Guthor. Tistator." She glanced at Kim, who nodded.

"Casoly!" Jo pointed her wand downward, gave it a flourish—and the chair disappeared.

At this the audience turned pin-drop quiet. It's working—it's working, Jo told herself. She and Kim just had to keep their heads, and not bobble anything. They could do it. They knew it well.

Standing as tall as possible, she circled the invisible chair with her hand extended toward it, palm out. "Super! Hang in there!" she murmured as she passed Kim, who was bending over the colored buttons.

"I'm ... I'm ready," Kim whispered back.

"Good. I am, too." Jo stopped beside the invisible chair. "Helon. Verf. Agla. Tetrogrammaton." She waved her wand.

"Tazphniel!" And the chair was back.

After heaving a great sigh, like the sound of a wave rustling over the sand, the audience started to clap, while Jo came to the front edge of the stage, rubbed her hands against her cloak, and took a deep bow. She had three things to do with TRANSMUTER, and one of them was behind her, a success.

"Thank you!" she shouted. "Thank you—*thank you!*" The applause died down. "This is hard work! I'm getting thirsty." She turned toward Kim again. "Have we something to drink?"

"Coffee?" The room was so quiet that even Kim's soft voice was clear.

"Perfect! Bring it on."

"Right here." Kim came forward with the percolator, which held the silks and Collapsible Dove.

Jo sniffed at it and rolled her eyes. "Peculiar!" she exclaimed. "The Power is strong!" Reaching in, she brought out a purple and a bright green silk, tied together, and then three more, which she piled on her stand.

"Ha! Beautiful!" She pulled out a yellow one and waved it, drew out a pink one and draped it over her arm, then produced four more and clapped her hand to her head in pretended astonishment. "What next?" She looked into the pot again, tugged out her largest yellow banner and last of all the Dove, which immediately swelled to its full size. The audience was still stone-quiet.

"Keep it up," she whispered to Kim, who came forward to pick up the coffeepot. "You're doing great!"

With a sweep of her arm, Jo pushed the silks off her stand into a heap on the floor—pink and yellow, blue and purple and green—and set the Dove on top. "Too many! Who needs all that?" she shouted. Shaking out TRANSMUTER's shawl, she tossed it on top of the pile and knelt beside it, folding its edge carefully away from the floor.

"Abac. Aldal. Hibac...." She recited the spell again and walked around the pile of silks, moving her wand slowly back and forth above them. Kim nodded.

"Casoly!" Jo brandished her wand—and the silks and shawl were gone. The audience drew breath in a long-drawn "Oh-h-h."

"Do you want them back?" she called out.

"Yes!" It was a roar.

"We'll try." She repeated the spell and looked at Kim, who nodded.

"Tzaphniel!" Jo waved her wand again. The pile returned, and the audience started to clap, while

someone at the rear shouted "Bravo!" Smiling, Jo wiped her sweaty hands against her thighs; the lights were hot.

And now was the final part, the scary part, for which she must be supercareful. "I'm cold!" She pretended to shiver as she picked up the shawl and draped it around her shoulders. "Got to get warm somehow. Where shall I go?"

She brushed back her hair and stood behind her magician's stand. Would the audience hear her heart thumping so? "Abac. Aldal. Hibac. Guthac. Tistator." She paused. "Not enough! She clapped her hand to her forehead, pretending to think. "Dalmaley."

Clasping the ends of the shawl in her hands, she walked in a circle.

"Lamack." She glanced at Kim, whose lips formed a soundless "Okay."

"Tetro-tetrogrammaton." She clutched the shawl around her.

"Casoly!"

At the familiar lurch and swoop, Jo clung tightly to the stand. For a moment the audience sat in stunned silence, then broke into a roar of delight. She looked at herself, and yes, her arms and legs were transparent and the bare floorboards showed through. She picked up the Unbeatable Drum and took it to Kim, holding it high so it seemed to float through the air.

"Nice and warm now!" she called out in a hollow, deep tone, as the audience became quiet again. She twirled the rope from the Strong Man's Secret so that it seemed to spin by itself. She jumped with it twice, then picked up the folding chair and carried it in a high circle, as if it had wings.

"Jo! Jo!" shouted Kim, pretending to be afraid.

"Want to sit down?" Jo set the chair beside Kim, who collapsed into it, with her arms hanging down.

"Jo! Where are you?" she squeaked.

"Right here beside you. Can't you tell?"

"Jo!" Kim squeaked again. "We want to see you! Please come back!"

"Okay!" Jo shouted. "I've had enough of this anyway. Are you ready?"

"All ready!" Kim struggled to her feet and took her place beside her table.

Deepening her voice still further, Jo picked up the chair to float it around the stage once more. "I'd like to see all of you again, and let you see me, too. Friendly-like," she shouted. "That'll take a *really super* spell." She set down the chair. "Helon. Verf. Agla. Tetrogrammaton." She drew a long, audible, hissing breath. "Pancia. Merroe."

She went to her stand, took firm hold with both hands, and braced her feet. This was it!

"Lamideck."

Although Kim had turned white, she gave Jo an almost inperceptible nod.

"Mitraton!" Another deep breath, and another nod.

"Tzaphniel!"

Jo felt a sickening plunge. The stage rocked. The sound of clapping came at her in a pulsating roar. The lights swooped crosswise in reckless circles and streaks, and the floor seemed to rise and fall like ocean waves. But she closed her eyes and held fast to the stand. She could feel herself swaying. The spinning slowed down. And then she was steadier—steadier—until the floor was solid and she could clearly see her hands, her feet, the front of her cloak.

"That's all, folks!" she shouted. Picking up the shawl, she held it in both hands while she and Kim bowed together to the sound of cheers. "Bravo!" "Hooray!" Even after the curtains closed, the applause continued until the girls stepped out in front again.

They had done it! They were a hit! Scarcely hearing the rest of the program, Jo repacked TRANSMUTER in the suitcase and as she worked she dreamed about herself, the Disappearing Conjurer, who performed for the president. For royalty. She'd make trips to China—Italy—Japan.

Afterward, when the program was over, she stood in a line with Kim and the other performers, the suitcase at her feet. "Oh, thank you! Thank you!" As people filed past, Jo shook hands that were soft and hands that were hard, hands that squeezed hers, hands that felt damp and cold. This was fun!

A bearded young reporter was there from the *Coastal Courier,* camera in hand. "A picture? Have to put a stunt like that on the front page!" He grinned as he set off a flash. "What's your system, anyway? Sure looked as if you were really gone."

"Just—a magic spell." Jo smiled at him as he moved on.

Next came a group of high-school students wanting autographs, and then a young women who introduced herself as Marcie Hays from Mitchell, a nearby town. "We're lining up talent for the Variety Show during our Festival of Kites, in June. Would you be interested?" she asked.

Jo caught her breath. Her first offer already! "I think so, if my parents will take us. They're in ..."

"Mom'll take us!" Kim interrupted in her most breathless voice. Pink-cheeked now and sparkling, she was chattering eagerly with everyone who came along.

"No need for that," the young women assured them. "We'll provide your transportation. And a performer's fee, of course. I'll contact you later." She jotted down Jo's telephone number.

One member of the audience was Mr. Smith, the drama coach from high school, who vigorously pumped her hand. "A fine act! Sometime I'd like to know how you concealed those objects—and even yourself. It looked like a genuine disappearance."

"It was the spell, of course!" Jo uttered the phrase she had said so many times.

"Yes. But magic aside, you have an authentic sense of timing. Have you thought about doing something with drama? We'll have a workshop in the park again this year, and present several plays. I'm sure you'd have some roles, if you care to try. Maybe as a comic?"

Even being called a comic didn't hurt now! Jo gave Mr. Smith a delighted smile and replied, "Oh— I'll be pretty busy. But thank you just the same."

"Well, keep it in mind." Mr. Smith moved on, while Jo turned toward an excited group of Merlins.

"We're so *proud* of you!" one of them said. "Especially the way you made the chair disappear. And *yourself!*"

"Yeah!" exclaimed another. "I'd like to do that, too—if I could."

"You could. All you need is . . ." Jo stopped in dismay. She'd been going to say that all they needed was the Trick! "All you need is lots of practice," she finished. "We worked hard."

"That's what it takes. Mr. Paisley told us so." Laughing, the Merlins went on, but for Jo a little of the evening's glamour was gone. *All you need is— the Trick.* She had almost said it. But it wasn't true! She'd figured out a really special act, and it was a sensation. *She* was good! She! Herself! Not just TRANSMUTER!

She was still feeling as if she had been scratched all over when she glanced down the line and saw Sidney, dressed in his best black and white checked suit and a red bow tie. Although Jo longed to run away and hide, she kept her feet planted firmly on the floor, and in a few minutes Sidney was there, holding out his hand.

"Stupendous, truly stupendous," he said, mustache quivering above a grin. "You've a bright future."

"Oh, thank you," Jo managed to reply.

"I want to talk with you about it." He had been shaking her hand, as everyone did, but instead of letting go, he continued to hold it fast.

"Yes ... well ... some other time." Jo tried to pull her hand away from his.

He gripped it with fingers that felt like iron. "I was really impressed." He grinned again, a wide grin that showed his gleaming teeth. "I've seldom seen a disappearing act quite like yours—although I've heard of them." He winked. "When we have more time, I'd like to find out all about it."

"Yes. Of course. But tonight ... pretty soon ... I have to leave!" Jo stammered. "Mrs. Forbes is waiting, and my brother is, too."

"To be sure. Have a good sleep, and dream about your splendid conjuring act. I'll see you another time." With another wink, Sidney let go her hand.

The crowd was thinner now, the last one in line being Mr. Paisley, shoulders bent and white hair curling over his collar. He was dressed in his best black suit, a little shiny at the edges, and wearing a blue necktie with a design of tiny white rabbits. "Miss Joanna!" he said, his eyes serious. "You surprised me."

Surprised him! thought Jo. Was that all he could say? Didn't he notice how she spoke out, and looked at her audience, just as he had taught her? Didn't he like it? "I tried to remember everything you said. Diction, and planning the act, and ..." She held out her hand.

He touched it briefly, but slipped her no joking surpises, no Anthony Mouse, no silks. His fingers were limp, and his eyes serious. "Yes, you remembered." His voice was low. "But you seem to have ... expanded a bit."

"I ... I guess I did." Jo plunged ahead. "Mr. Paisley, they've asked me to be in the Mitchell Festival of Kites. That's ... nice ... don't you think so?"

"And you accepted?"

"Of course!" Jo felt a lump in her throat. Wasn't he her friend anymore? Wasn't he glad she had done so well? "That last part of my act—it's the trick you sold me."

"I remember." Mr. Paisley gave her a long, sober look over the tops of his spectacles. "A piece from the Capricorn, I believe. And, apparently, it has done all that you hoped."

"Well—yes." Was he angry? Mr. Paisley, who had always been her friend? Why hadn't she told him about the secret drawer, the day she bought TRANS-MUTER? She'd been sneaky, and Mr. Paisley must have figured it out. "I should have explained," she blurted. "But I was in a hurry. I've been so busy all week, and I was thinking about this show. I wanted ..."

"I understand. We won't worry about that. But Joanna, I am concerned about your Trick. If you lose it, what will you have left?"

What did he mean? "I'll never lose it! I'll keep it forever," Jo protested, trying not to think about her messy room, after it had been searched. "It's the best I've ever had."

"Perhaps ... perhaps. But how will you keep it safe? More important ..." He rubbed his fingers across his forehead, and the lines around his mouth deepened. "How will you keep yourself safe? If something happens to it while you're under the spell—what then?"

"I'll watch it! Every second! See? I have it with me now, here in the suitcase."

"I hope you're right, Joanna, but I don't feel easy. I can't forget that your Trick came from a fellow who wanted to make a quick fortune. A loner. Not very scrupulous. It doesn't seem ... quite ...

suitable for you." He brushed his fingers across his forehead, closing his eyes as if they hurt. "I blame myself. I should have made sure what you'd found, when you asked to buy the Trick."

"It will be all right! I know it will!"

"Let us hope so." Forehead still creased with a worried pucker, Mr. Paisley shuffled away.

Jo scarcely listened to Kim's chatter or Mrs. Forbes's admiring remarks as they gathered up the rest of their gear and drove home in the station wagon. "Just tired, I guess," she said when Woody asked her what was wrong.

Everything had been so wonderful—until it was spoiled. What did Sidney mean, winking and wanting to see her? And Mr. Paisley had ruined everything. Didn't he want her to have any fun? Why had he asked those awful questions that were nagging and nagging her and wouldn't stop? *If you lose it, what will you have left? How will you keep it safe?*

She'd put on the best act of her entire life, and now . . . now . . . Jo straightened her shoulders. She wouldn't think about Sid or about Mr. Paisley either. She was Joanna Rodgers, Magician. And she was famous, almost.

The Druid's Cave Again

WHEN JO WOKE UP THE NEXT MORNING, HALF of her wanted to sing and shout so everybody in Madrona could hear. She had been in the talent show, her act had gone well, and she had an offer for another performance already. It was just as she had hoped.

But her other half was uneasy. *How will you keep it safe?* Mr. Paisley had asked. *If you lose it, what will you have left?* Of course those were ridiculous questions; but she couldn't bear to have him angry, so she'd go to the Cave this very morning and explain, and then they'd be friends again. With that decided, she ran downstairs, humming under her breath.

Mrs. Forbes had cooked breakfast—tough scrambled eggs, watery around the edges—and she chattered as she passed them to Jo. "I'm *so proud* of you, dear. You were every bit as good as the magician last week on channel six. The way you disappeared right in front of us! It almost seemed like real magic!"

"Well ..." Jo stopped. Was that all *anybody* had noticed? "We practiced a lot." She looked toward Woody, who snickered and rolled his eyes.

"You bowled them over," he agreed. "You've got a *real* Trick."

Jo flashed him an indignant glance, but he only broadened his grin and put two slices of bread into the toaster. "Magicians can do surprising things," she said stiffly. Nobody except Mr. Paisley had any idea how hard she had worked.

Right after breakfast she stuffed TRANSMUTER into her backpack, which was the safest way to carry it, and rode down the hill with Mrs. Forbes, who was going early to polish some lamps. Old Main Street was still asleep, drowsing in the still air. The shops had their shutters closed, the sun was low, casting long shadows, and white-breasted gulls were sitting solemnly on pilings in the bay.

Since it was early and the door of the Cave was locked, Jo went into the park and strolled down a side path bordered by clumps of rhododendron and salmon berries higher than her head. At the rocky shore, where the Neck was narrow, she sat down on a log to watch the tide pouring past, a steel-gray river on its way to the sea. A drift log swept by, with an elbow-shaped broken branch jutting up from the waves. A fishing boat blew a hollow note as it set out, decks heaped with orange nets.

Jo set her backpack on the ground beside her, removed TRANSMUTER, and took the shawl and control box out of the leather case to look them over again. Just as she was refolding the shawl, she heard steps behind her, and turned around to see Sidney striding down the path, jacket unbuttoned and flapping around him.

"Ah-ha! Our youthful conjurer!" He broke into a broad grin. "I've been pining for a chat, and when I saw you pass my window, I seized the golden chance. We won't be disturbed here." He stopped just before he reached Jo, and clasped his hands together. "*Lovely* day, isn't it. Calm. Serene."

Calm! Serene! thought Jo, as she stuffed the leather case into the backpack and snatched up the shawl and control box. "You!" she exploded, as she jumped to her feet. "You broke into my room!"

"I?" Sidney arched his eyebrows in astonishment. "Whatever gave you such a bizarre idea? I'd never be so intrepid."

"Your friend, then. That ... that ..."

He laughed again. "McElroy? Breaking and entering? How *hilarious*! He might have arranged it, because he likes to have things go his way. But no, he'd never stoop to such a job himself."

Jo wanted to run, but Sidney was in the path, and it was narrow, so she stood fast and slung the backpack onto her shoulder.

"As I said before, you had a splendid act. Riveted us to our seats. Enthralled us. Quite," he continued. "Your device is . . . beyond price." He moved closer, and Jo backed a step away, clutching the control box and shawl.

"Now, now! I don't bite, you know." Sidney moved ahead, but slowly, one step at a time. "I only want to make an offer. For you, the device is just a trick. Limited value. But I have a use for it, and I'll be glad to take it off your hands. For a good price, too."

Keep him talking! Watch for a chance to run! Jo told herself. "You'd really like it?" she asked, trying to put on a friendly smile. "Do you want to . . . to be a magician?"

"Magician? Prestidigitator?" Sidney threw back his head with a bray of laughter. "One of those? Not me. But McElroy will buy it from me, and he'll pay me well."

"Why? What does he want it for?"

Sidney raised his shoulders and turned his palms out, in an exaggerated shrug. "Good question—but I can't answer it. He hasn't seen fit to confide in me, and I haven't asked him to. He'll pay cash. The definitive factor."

Sidney was standing in the path, which was so narrow that he almost touched the rhododendrons on both sides. Jo couldn't possibly get by, and even if she did, she wasn't sure she could outrun him. But the control box was in her left hand, the shawl was draped over her arm, and—yes! *She could work it by touch, without looking at it, so he wouldn't notice! She had done it before!*

"I don't ... quite ... understand." She kept her voice steady while she curled her fingers over the colored buttons and risked one quick glance, to make sure the control box was right-side up. "A lot of cash?" she asked.

"Well-l-l, yes. Enough to feed my hungry creditors, and then some. With a bit left over for you. Say ..." Sidney stroked his straggly mustache. "How would you like some cash of your own, enough to buy the best device in Mr. Paisley's stock? Maybe the Changing Chest. It's a dandy."

"The Chest? It's good, all right." Jo felt for the green button, fourth from the left. "But, Sid, that doesn't seem like very much." Staring straight straight into Sidney's eyes, she pressed green. "This is a special Trick, worth more than that."

Yellow. Red. *Don't hurry. Move as little as possible, so he won't guess.*

"I'm astounded! Disillusioned. Stupefied. My bubble is pricked. I didn't think a charming girl would be so greedy!" Sidney clucked his tongue in mock reproach. "But just to please an old friend—suppose I up the ante. All the tricks you could use for a long time to come. Levitators. Escape trunks. Enough to set up you for the professional stage." He took a step toward her, and Jo edged away.

"Professional!" she said, not looking down. Orange. *Careful now. Not too fast.* "That sounds like quite a lot!"

"You'd better believe it!" he exclaimed.

Yellow. Jo shook her head with what she hoped was a puzzled frown. "But still, it's just magic. Maybe I'll get tired of it and want to do something else."

Sidney drew his eyebrows together in pretended reproach. "Jo, Jo! Fickle woman! Even you! And I thought magic was your life!" He shook his head. "You're a hard bargainer, for such a lissome lass. But you'll be wanting college some day, a smart girl like you. How about enough cash to cover your expenses, anywhere you'd like?"

Red! Red! She'd finished! Instead of answering, Jo touched her arm, to be sure the shawl was there, then held her breath and pressed the final button.

Black. She felt the tingly jolt. The ground seemed to buckle under her feet, and a fallen log showed clearly through her knees. She swayed but didn't fall, while Sidney's eyes widened and his jaw dropped open.

"Ul-l-lp!" Catching his breath, he lunged toward

the place where Jo was standing, but she slipped among the rhododendrons and glanced back in time to see him snatch at empty air. Brush cracked and branches swayed as she plunged through them, with Sidney almost at her heels, following the sound. As soon as possible she circled back to the main path, where she could move quietly, and from there she tiptoed into an open space. Breathing carefully, she stood there motionless while Sidney passed her, almost close enough to touch.

As soon as he was out of sight, Jo crept out of her niche, remaining invisible because she felt safer that way. When she reached Main Street, she found that shops were beginning to open, so she hurried to the Cave, ran up the steps, and pounded on the door.

Mr. Paisley opened it. "Hello? Is somebody there?" he asked, with one hand on the knob.

"Yes. It's me!" she replied between gasps.

"Joanna? Into your act?" Mr. Paisley narrowed his faded eyes as he looked in her general direction. "Well, come along and tell me about it." He held the door open for a moment, then asked, with another puzzled glance, "Are you inside?"

"I'm here."

"Very well. And Joanna, I have my stove going, so let's enjoy it." After relocking the door, he put the keys into his pocket and led her to the rear of the shop, where he put a fresh chunk of wood onto the fire. "Please, Joanna, take a seat. And I'd feel considerably more comfortable if I could see you," he murmured, sinking into one of the chairs.

"Of course. I'll only be a minute. Violet. Indigo...." Jo sat down and said the colors aloud, working her way through the list until she was almost through. "Mr. Paisley, this next part isn't very easy, but don't worry. It won't last," she whispered. "White." She felt the jolt. The room spun, and Mr. Paisley seemed to have turned into two men, both foreheads creased with worry, while Jo clung fast to the arms of the chair and shut her eyes against the dizzy streaks of color.

"Easy there!" he touched her knee with his hand, wrinkled knuckles standing out knobby under the papery skin. "You're all right, Joanna. You're here."

The streaks became smaller—stopped—and everything was steady again. "Yes. I'm okay now. And Mr. Paisley ..." Jo blurted out her story all in a rush, forgetting her plans to tell it completely and logically, right from the beginning. "And Sidney wants my Trick," she finished. "He found me in the park, so I turned myself invisible."

Mr. Paisley listened quietly until she was through. "Sidney wants it? Hmm," he said then, drawing his mouth into a grim line. "And if he'd caught you before you undid the spell? What then?"

Jo gasped. "I ... oh! Maybe he wouldn't have turned me back! Ever!" She inched forward in her chair, closer to the fire. "But I got away! I knew I'd be all right as soon as I came to the Cave."

Mr. Paisley looked severely at her, over the tops of his spectacles. "Your Trick—whatever it may be—is powerful stuff, Joanna. You mustn't forget that," he said.

"Oh, I won't. And . . ." Jo gulped and started over. "Mr. Paisley, I never did tell you exactly where I found it."

Taking a deck of cards from his pocket, he shuffled them mechanically, as if twiddling his thumbs. Except for the whirr of cards and snap of the fire, the Cave was quiet.

Jo continued. "It was in the desk—I told you that. But I didn't explain that it was in . . . in a secret drawer." Stopping and starting and cringing with every word, she told him the rest of the tale.

"So that's the way it was," he said then, sounding calm, although he wasn't smiling. "I'm glad you told me, Joanna. It clears the air."

Jo caught her breath. "Mr. Paisley, I was asked last night to be in the Variety Show for the Festival of Kites, in the summer. That would be fun."

"I'm sure it would." He continued to shuffle the cards.

She plunged in again. "Mr. Paisley, after the show, you asked me what I'd have left, if I lost it. What did you mean?"

"Don't you know?"

Jo bristled. Didn't he realize that she'd been asking herself this question, over and over again! "I'd have everything left that I ever had—wouldn't I?"

"How many new tricks have you learned, or tried to learn, this week?" he asked.

"I was . . . we were pretty busy."

"If you hadn't had your Trick, might you have attempted something else?"

Jo thought through the last few days. "Maybe . . . maybe the Zombie Balls. Or the Journey Through Space. Kim wanted me to finish learning them."

"Did you try?"

"Well, no."

He smiled, a wry little smile, not his familiar, crinkly, kindly one. "Why not?"

"We didn't have time. And we didn't need them, anyway, because we had . . . we had . . ." Running down, Jo sat in miserable silence.

At this Paisley riffled through the cards once more and handed them to her. "Joanna, remember the Double Fan? It's difficult, but you had mastered it well. Show it to me."

Jo looked at him for a moment, then shuffled the cards; but they seemed stiff and awkward, not at all as she remembered them. "They don't feel like mine," she complained.

"They're standard, and yours are, too," he said. "Go ahead. Try it."

"All right." Biting her lip, Jo gave the cards the

flip she had learned; but instead of spreading evenly as they were meant to, they slid through her fingers and fell onto the floor. "It didn't . . . quite . . . work," she faltered.

"No."

She felt almost angry. "I know why! You don't have to tell me. It's because I was so *busy*! Because I didn't *practice*!" She glared at him. "I can figure that much out!"

Mr. Paisley sighed. "That's right. You see, Joanna, your Transmuter requires courage, but very little skill. While you are focused on it, you aren't developing your talent—and you do have talent. You're sacrificing it for instant success, which is a poor trade."

At this, as if it had dropped down from the ceiling and hit her on the head, Jo found herself face to face with the idea that had been dogging her. Even though she'd been a rousing success, TRANSMUTER had done it, not she herself, Joanna Rodgers. Any of the Merlins—Kim—even Woody—could work the Trick just as well as she could. She hadn't been wonderful at all.

Moreover, as long as she had TRANSMUTER, she wouldn't learn anything new. After a while it would be the only trick she had mastered; and if she lost it, she wouldn't have anything left, not even her own self-respect. That was what Mr. Paisley's questions had meant.

She clutched TRANSMUTER tightly in both hands. "I guess it isn't so great, after all. And I feel awful, getting it the way I did," she said, feeling frightened and confused. "I'll give it back."

He shook his head. "I don't want it, Joanna. It's your Trick. I sold it to you. You know now what it means, the good and the bad, and you must make up your own mind how to handle it."

Jo didn't answer. She was staring at the fire when she heard a key in the front door and turned around to see Sidney striding into the shop. "Ah-ha—our young necromancer! We meet again!" Hair straggling over his forehead, he came toward them with long steps. "I met Jo in the park," he continued. "She played a little joke on me." He shook his head at her and grinned. "But no hard feelings. I'm interested in that device of hers, and I think she'd like to unload it."

Mr. Paisley made a tent of his fingers.

"You have a good trick, Jo," Sidney continued with a wheedling smile, "but it's hardly suitable for a kid. So I'll raise my price, to take it off your hands. A full half of McElroy's offer."

Jo glowered at the shawl, lying across her knees with the control box on top. She'd been hiding those wretched things in her boot for days, so nobody could steal them. She'd hung onto them like glue, every second of the talent show. Her room had been broken into. She'd forgotten how to do her best card trick. Dodged her friends' questions. And it was all on account of that miserable TRANSMUTER.

Miserable? TRANSMUTER?

Yes! That's what it was! Miserable! And dangerous! If Sidney got his hands on it, and sold it to that man, he could use it for smuggling! For robbery! It could cause somebody to be killed! That awful Trick would damage her and everything it touched. She didn't want it, and she didn't want McElroy to have it, either.

She dropped down beside the stove, jerked open the iron door, and blinked at the surge of hot air.

"Hey! Stop it! You idiot!" Sidney flung himself toward Jo, but she hurled the control box and shawl onto the flame, and slammed the door.

"Imbecile! Ninny! Birdbrain! Do you realize . . . ?" Sidney stood above her, clenching and unclenching his fists. "A fortune, that's what it was worth. And you've *burned it up!*"

"Good!" Jo could see TRANSMUTER through the glass panels, the corners of its control box already curling and the shawl sending up flames of gold and green, scarlet and blue. *Destroyed by heat,* the directions had said. *Disintegrates at temperatures above* 110°. It was really gone.

"You moved fast, Joanna. A noble act," said Mr. Paisley.

"Noble! Faugh! She's a born fool!" Sidney spun on his heel and stomped away. In a moment Jo heard the jingle of the bell, the squeak of the door, a resounding slam, and then the Cave was still.

She returned to her chair and watched the flames, as TRANSMUTER was turned to ash. The leather case was empty now, as empty as she felt herself. She had made a big, black, yawning hole in her summer, and nothing was left to fill it up.

"What are you going to do next?" Mr. Paisley asked in a few minutes. "Have you plans?"

"Nope," she replied. "Just ... nothing special. They won't want me now for the Festival of Kites."

For the first time that morning Mr. Paisley smiled his own warm smile. "They might. You must tell the young woman—Miss Hays ... ?"

"Hays, yes. Marcie Hays."

"You must explain, of course, how much your act has changed, but you needn't tell the whole story." His smile broadened. "I doubt that it will matter. You have a very funny performance, Joanna, with some excellent deceptions, and you'll have time to work it out further. Any audience would be pleased."

"Well, maybe." If Mr. Paisley liked it, that helped a little.

Smiling, he held out his hand, and he was holding Anthony Mouse. "For you," he said. "To keep."

"Oh!" Jo stroked its fur and joggled its foreleg,

and its whiskers twitched. She pressed its side, and it squeaked. *"Thank* you. I *love* him! I'll never forget you gave him to me, and I'll keep him forever."

Mr. Paisley's smile grew broader, crinkling his whole face. "He'll be useful to you, Joanna. He fascinates children. And I need a summer assistant. In the park."

Jo turned rigid. Had she heard it right? "You mean . . . ?"

"Yes. I'm offering you the job." Mr. Paisley nodded. "A chance at the Magicians' Fair, too, if you want it."

"But . . . but . . . I thought you were mad at me."

"Not angry, Joanna. Never that, although for a while I was doubtful. You were wrapped up in a gimmick, vulnerable, unwilling to learn. In that condition, you wouldn't have been much help to my young students. Nor could I have presented you to them as an example."

Jo clutched the Mouse so tightly she dented its stuffed white sides, and its whiskers twitched again.

Mr. Paisley continued. "But now you are the old Joanna once more. So—are you interested?"

"Interested! Oh-h-h!" This was almost as big a thrill as when she first set off the Trick. *Almost* as big? It was twice as big! Ten times! A hundred!

"I think you'll like working with children, and it's only a few hours a day. There'll also be time for a play or two. I heard the coach asking you to enroll."

"I'll ... well ..." In her mind Jo saw the stage of the summer theater, with herself on it, playing a role. Maybe that would be fun. "Yes! I'll try out, and see if I can get a part."

She felt herself growing lighter, as if she was invisible again, but when she looked down, there she was—arms, legs, all of her, the same old Jo as always. She wanted to sing and shout, jump up and dance a jig. A few minutes ago the summer had stretched before her, an enormous, empty, echoing hole, but suddenly it was full and overflowing. She'd have the classes in the park, with little kids to talk to about magic. She'd go to the Magicians' Fair. Perhaps be in a play.

"I think I'll tackle something hard!" she exclaimed. "Maybe the Zombie Balls. I think the children would like them. I'll call up Kim this very day."

She could hardly wait.